ALL THE TRUTHS

RINA KENT

To those who stand tall.

AUTHOR NOTE

Hello reader friend,

If you haven't read my books before, you might not know this, but I write darker stories that can be upsetting and disturbing. My books and main characters aren't for the faint of heart.

All The Truths is the second book of a duet and is NOT standalone.

Lies & Truths Duet:
#1 *All The Lies*
#2 *All The Truths*

Don't forget to Sign up to Rina Kent's Newsletter for news about future releases and an exclusive gift.

FOREWARD

Quick note,

These special edition covers are for all the lovers of spice who prefer "Safe for work" covers! Enjoy!

XOXO,
Rina

The truth doesn't set you free.

Revenge shouldn't be rushed. It needs to be savored.

Reina ruined my life and it's only fair I ruin hers back.

Or that was the plan.

That was before she got under my skin and flowed into my blood.

Life as we know it crashes and burns.

All we have left is revenge.

Or is it?

PLAYLIST

"Illuminated"—Hurts
"Infinite"—Silverstein & Aaron Gillespie
"Divide"—Bastille
"Good Lesson"—Bastille
"Wherever You Are"—Kodaline
"Call Me"—Shinedown
"State of My Head"—Shinedown
"Kill Our Way to Heaven"—Michl
"Emperor's New Clothes"—Panic! At The Disco
"No Shame"—5 Seconds of Summer
"Empty Thoughts"—Glass Tides
"Death of Me"—SAINT PHNX
"Willow Tree"—Twin Wild
"Wrong"—Depeche Mode
"Running From My Shadow"—Mike Shinoda & grandson
"I Found"—Amber Run
T"he Unknown"—Crossfade
"Just Give Me a Reason"—Pink & Nate Ruess
"What Have You Done"—Within Temptation & Keith
Caputo
"Roots"—In This Moment
"Wasting My Time"—Default
"The Very Last Time"—Bullet For My Valentine
"Haemorrhage"—Fuel
"Love Falls"—HELLYEAH
"Some Kind of Disaster"—All Time Low

ALL THE TRUTHS

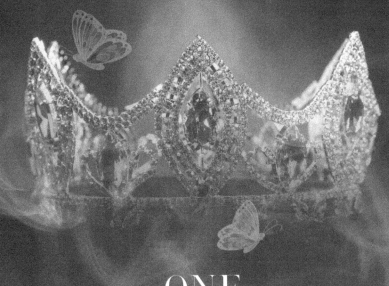

ONE

Reina

The night of the assault

L ife is unfair.
Its parallel lines and never-crossing patterns are like a curse.

No matter how much you run away from it, you always get pulled back.

Friday night lights fill the stadium as my squad's members smile and jump. The crowd's noise is like a rush of adrenaline for both the cheerleaders and the football players.

A small smile tugs on my lips as I stop near the exit and throw one last glance behind me, at Bree and Prescott, Lucy and Naomi, Owen and Seb.

And everyone else.

I never thought I would miss them, but then again, the whole robotic act was just that: an act. I never once thought they weren't important, but I was a professional at making them believe they weren't.

My gaze strays up of its own accord, to the spectators—the section for players' families.

That's where he always sits. In his closed-up, black mind, he still considers Owen and Sebastian family.

Which can never be said about me.

My fingers snake to my bracelet, feeling around the dainty material as I roam the crowd.

I know I won't find him, but I still search anyway; that says something about my desperation.

It says something about how dysfunctional we are.

I wish this had started three years ago, but it's been going on since Uncle Alex and Dad decided we were to be engaged.

Our relationship has been wrong and refused to be right ever since.

We just keep missing each other, over and over again.

Then he told me those words, the ones that shattered the remains of my heart into tiny, bloody pieces, impossible to collect or to touch.

There has been a constant ache in my chest since I finally realized the painful truth: we live in parallel lines. Our worlds are never meant to cross.

We were never meant to be.

Giving up on finding him in the crowd, I spin around and walk the long empty tunnel. The cheers and the music eventually fade, turning into nothingness.

With every step I take, my spirit loses balance. My limbs tremble as if begging me to go back in there, search for him, tell him what I couldn't all these years.

No.

It's over.

Everything is over.

Now, I have to save the only other person who matters more than I do.

I retrieve my phone and pull up Instagram. It doesn't take me long to find the conversation from a year ago. I wish I could've gone one more time or told the jerk these words in person, but despite my tough act, I'm a coward in so many ways.

I just know how to hide my cowardice well.

For a long time, I learned how to turn weakness into a strong façade, something solid and hard no one would suspect.

With trembling fingers, I type.

Reina-Ellis: I won't meet you again.

The reply is immediate. Sometimes, I get the feeling he's never there, and others—like now—it's almost as if he's breathing down my neck.

Cloud003: Nice try, my slut.

Reina-Ellis: I mean it. I'm turning the page and you chose not to be part of it. I know you're blocking any feelings you have for me and I understand. I probably should've done the same. I'm sorry and goodbye.

As I hit send, my eyes blur, and I close them to fight the onslaught.

It's all over now.

All the bad blood and unsaid words.

All the secrets and lies.

It's…over.

There's no reply—not that I expected one. He's a jerk that way, always making me wonder what he's thinking.

I hope it'll stop with this goodbye, but I doubt it will.

This thing is already flowing in my blood, and unlike common belief around Blackwood College, I do bleed, both physically and emotionally.

I've just mastered the art of deception and don't show it.

With one last touch to my bracelet, I forge ahead.

Tonight, I'm leaving everything behind and reuniting with the one person who always loved me unconditionally.

The one who gave me their life.

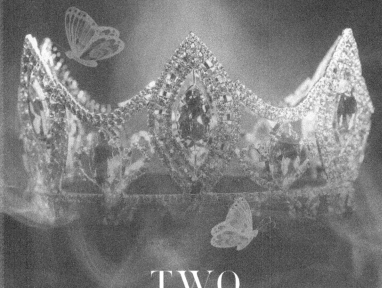

TWO

Reina
Present

Asher's silhouette becomes a blur as I struggle to catch my breath.

There's something paralyzing about pain. It's not the agony itself but the brain's reaction to being metaphorically stabbed.

It shuts down at the onslaught and chooses numbness instead, because sometimes, being numb is the only way to survive.

I wish it were physical pain. I wish it were that assault and the agony at the back of my neck and shoulders each time I moved.

At least back then, I lived with the belief that it would soon go away.

This pain won't.

It's at its rawest, truest form.

My thighs still ache from how Asher took me last night.

My insides are still sore from his touch, how he filled me, how he kissed me and stretched me whole.

A few moments ago, my heart was soaring, almost hitting the ceiling with all the butterflies. *Stupid* little butterflies.

They're slaughtered now, leaving blood and goo in their wake.

As I pull my trembling legs to my chest, I can hear it loud and clear: the breaking of a heart. The smash, the fall. I can almost see the pieces surrounding me like broken glass.

And it's all because of the man in the sharp suit standing in front of the pole.

The man who only approached me for revenge.

I trusted him. I was *falling* for him.

I ignored all the signs and my instinct and went to him. I considered him my savior when he's been my Grim Reaper all along.

Logically, I should stand up and go there. I should pull him by the shoulder, slap him across the face, and ask him why he did that to me—to *us*.

Tears well in my eyes at the mere thought. I can't possibly face him without breaking at his feet.

He'll taunt me and call me a monster; he'll tell me it's all my fault. I can't take that right now. My armor has chipped and is now heaped in a useless pile amongst the broken pieces.

So I do the one thing I can at this moment. My nails dig into the dirt as I use it to rise to my feet.

There's something so utterly hard about standing up after a fall. The ground keeps pulling me down as if not willing to let me go. It's gravity, I know that, but my brain is unable to process that fact right now.

It takes me long seconds, but I manage to stand up on unsteady feet. I don't look at Asher—not even one glance.

If I do, I'll make the broken pieces worse. I'll soak them with blood, bury them in my chest, and it'll be an unsalvageable mess.

I take one step after another, putting one foot in front of the other.

One step.

Two steps.

I can do this. I can walk.

It takes me what seems like an eternity to reach the entrance. It's empty, desolate and…wrong.

That sensation from the hospital returns with a vengeance.

Wrong.

Everything is just so fucking wrong, from the house to the hollowness to the damn air.

Jason stands at the front, leaning against the double doors. His developed arms are crossed over his chest as he watches me with furrowed brows.

He knew all along.

That's why he warned me through Cloud003's Instagram account. If I'd paid enough attention, I probably could've done something about it.

I could've stopped myself before I fell this deep into Asher's trap.

Problem is, I didn't even feel it when I was lured in. I couldn't smell the scheme or sense the manipulations. I suspected him, but never enough to think he was after my life—literally.

I only felt the push when I fell. I only registered the fall when all the pieces scattered around me under that tree.

"Are you okay?" Jason asks slowly, but he doesn't move from his spot.

My feet come to a screeching halt at the step. When I meet his gaze, my movements are slow and almost robotic. In my attempts to stop myself from crying, I've turned numb.

The hot sun above might as well become a gray cloud. I feel nothing, see nothing, and smell nothing. The world has suddenly become colorless, and I have no idea if I want the colors back.

"Ah, shit." He rubs the back of his neck and approaches me slowly, as if I'm an injured animal. "Did Asher say something? I knew that asshole would step on you."

"Why didn't you tell me before?" I don't recognize my voice; it's neutral and dead, colorless like the world surrounding me.

He rubs his nape again, appearing uncomfortable. "Asher threatened me and my mom. She'll have nowhere to go if Alex fires her, so we have to stay here until I secure my position in the NFL."

"What made you change your mind?"

"I can't keep watching you consider him a hero when he's your worst villain." His tone hardens with every word. "He never cared about you, Reina. Not once in his selfish, fucked-up existence did Asher Carson look at you like he gives two fucks about your wellbeing."

My brows furrow.

Yes, Asher might have only approached me for revenge, and he's always been his own brand of asshole, but I saw those small gestures...the way his eyes softened, the show of affection in his green gaze, the tightening of his jaw afterward as if he didn't want to care.

It doesn't matter, though, does it?

None of it erases what he did. His intention was loud and clear on the roof, in the classroom, and in the locker room.

He wanted to kill me.

Don't they say actions speak louder than words?

I've witnessed his actions. Hell, I can still feel those creepy vibes down to my bones.

"Tell me everything you know, Jace." I meet his kind brown gaze with my determined one.

My brain is telling me to retreat to my room, hide under the covers, and cry—but my sheets still smell like him from yesterday. Hell, my entire body does.

I'm still sore from him, still full of him in ways even I don't want to admit.

Besides, if I give the gloomy cloud any freedom, it'll just take over and leave me with nothing but depression and dark thoughts.

My best bet is to know what I've done. There's nothing scarier than ignorance. It slowly creeps under your skin and eats you alive, and when you decide to act, it's already too late.

I'm solving this before it turns unresolvable.

Jason cocks his head to the side. "Follow me."

I don't question and walk behind him as he heads to the pool house.

His shoulders become my focus as I try to walk right. My brain keeps pulling me in different directions. One part wants to run back to Asher and demand the truth from him. The other part is letting the gloomy cloud whisper nasty things in my brain.

See? You're nothing.

Why don't you follow Arianna and just die?

No one cares about you.

The sound of a closing door shuts those demons up. I didn't realize we were in the pool house until Jason locks the double doors.

Something is secretive enough to warrant this, I suppose.

"I knew this day would come." He speaks as he heads toward the TV on the opposite wall. "I knew I'd have a use for this." He retrieves a flash drive from his pocket and hooks it into the TV, cocking his head back. "Are you ready?"

"For what?"

"This footage will give you an idea of what you need to know."

My palms turn clammy as I slowly nod.

He motions at the cushions lined up in front of the TV. "You might want to sit down, Reina."

I approach them at a snail's pace, suddenly not sure if this is the place I want to be in.

Before I can voice my thoughts, Jason plays the video.

The footage's angle is sideways, and the quality is grainy like those old security videos. It's almost as if it's been recorded in secret.

There's no audio.

It's just a frame of Asher and me standing in front of the locker room. The football team's, I think. I'm wearing a blue cheerleading uniform and Asher has a blue Tigers jacket on, which means it's from high school time.

Although I can't hear any words, I can feel the maliciousness on my skin. Asher appears pissed off, his jaw clenching and his hands balled into fists by his sides. I, on the other hand, seem cool. My arms are crossed over my chest and my expression is robotic, like the one from the fake pictures on the internet.

As he grits his teeth, forcing words out, I stand there un-moving. Silent. No reaction.

I'm entranced by the scene: the volatile tension in his body, the complete relaxation of mine.

Only, am I really relaxed?

I tilt my head to the side, watching closely. From the out-side looking in, I appear completely unaffected. However, my nails dig into my arms. It's not hard enough to draw attention, but it's there. I'm doing that to rein it in. I can tell without hav-ing to remember that particular scene.

But what was I reining in? My reaction? My emotions?

What exactly were you hiding, Old Reina?

Asher pushes past me on his way out. I stumble backward with the force of it, but I hold my ground. As he disappears from the scene, I stare directly at the camera. It's a full-on glare, one that's meant to dissect souls and ruin lives.

It's the harsh Reina.

The Reina no one fucked with.

The screen goes black right after.

I continue staring at it as if Asher and I were still there.

"That's only a fraction of your relationship." Jason brings my attention back to him. "You were never actually together."

My gaze slides from the black screen to his face. "Who re-corded that?"

He pauses as if it's the last question he expected I'd ask. I want to know who I looked at with that icy stare. There was someone who filmed something they shouldn't have, and I want to know if they paid for intruding on my privacy.

"Someone from the football team? I'm not sure. I found it online a few years ago."

"You keep all videos you find online?"

"The ones concerning you, yes. We're friends, princess, remember?"

"No, I don't remember. That's the whole thing, Jace." My voice is resigned more than anything. "What do you know about my involvement with Arianna?"

Asher and I might have had problems, but they weren't so huge to the point he'd have murderous intentions toward me. Something tells me all of this started after Arianna's death.

Jason abandons his position near the TV and flops beside me. His gaze gets lost in the black screen like mine was earlier. "You were friends."

"Define friends."

"From the outside? Best friends. She never did anything without you by her side. You were her role model and she relied on you so much, to the point Asher didn't like it."

The sound of his name slaughters me all over again.

My lashes flutter over my cheeks as I fight the onslaught of pain hitting me out of nowhere. Those broken pieces are now trying to puncture what remained of my heart, as if demanding that everything should be left for dead.

"What changed?" My voice is higher than normal. "Earlier you said she hurt me and I didn't hold back."

"I'm not sure either." He lifts a shoulder. "All I know is that Arianna was acting weird right before her suicide."

"Weird how?"

"She clung to you more. Asher distanced himself from you more than usual. You were miserable and appeared to have a million thoughts going on in your head."

"You said I drove her to suicide—how?"

"Those are Asher's words, not mine. Apparently, Arianna said you were to blame before she jumped."

A soft gasp tears out of me, and my voice turns haunted. "I was to blame how?"

"No idea, but Asher believes it as if it's his religion. He fought with Alex about it right after Arianna's death. He demanded his father sever all ties with you, but he wasn't having it and told him to stop being irrational."

My chest squeezes at the kindness from the man who's filled the role of father since Dad passed away. "Alex didn't believe him?"

Jason shakes his head.

"How about you?" My voice is so filled with hope it's pathetic.

"It doesn't matter what I believe."

"It matters to me." If Jace is Cloud003, he's possibly the only friend I have in this pile of chaos, and right now, I need someone I can lean on.

"Of course not, Reina. There might have been disagreements before her death, but you loved Arianna as if she were your sister. She was the only one you never acted snobby or robotic with."

"Then how come Asher believes I'd hurt her?"

"I don't know. Honestly, there's no proof of what he said. He was the only one on the roof when Arianna committed suicide, so there are no other witnesses. I think he's only using his sister's death to inflict pain on you. Since he couldn't get rid of you before, that opportunity was golden for him."

My palms turn sweaty as I clasp my hands together.

No.

As monstrous as Asher's grudge is, it's real and tangible. I saw the intensity of it in his green eyes and tasted it on my tongue.

He didn't make it up. He really thinks I had something to do with Arianna's suicide.

Now, I must figure out a way to prove my innocence, and I need to find it quick.

Judging from Asher's pace with things, I won't be so lucky next time he comes back for my soul.

I meet Jason's gaze. "Yesterday you said something about things escalating before Izzy stopped you."

"Yeah." He rubs the back of his neck. "I think he's after your life, Reina. Those attacks were only a preparation for the grand finale. Next time, he'll force you to jump off a roof like Arianna did."

I gulp at the thought, not because I'm scared, but more because of how that possibility hurts.

"Do you think he's the one who beat me up in the forest?" I ask.

"Probably."

The remaining part of my heart shrinks and turns into stone.

Asher took everything from me.

Maybe I have taken everything from him, too.

Now we have nothing.

Don't they say those who have nothing to lose are the scariest?

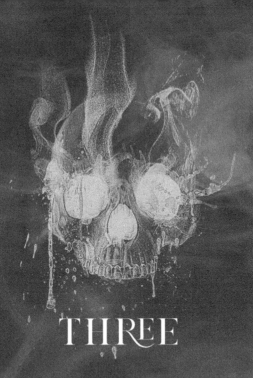

THREE

Asher

L ife is strange.

One day it's all unicorns and rainbows, and the next, it's a straight-up trip to hell.

It's fight or flight.

It's kill or be killed.

I straighten in front of Ari's grave, one hand clutching the other in front of me.

Arianna Carson, beloved daughter and sister.

Each word is a ruthless stab. The sentence is as gruesome as if it were written in blood.

She died so young, in her prime years, seventeen going on eighteen.

Her smile is starting to fade from my memories. It crashed and burned that day three years ago.

All I can see is her tear-streaked face, the trembling of her lips, and the white dress that flew in the wind behind her as she stood on the edge.

Her face was pale as she shook like a leaf and confessed the words that killed me on the spot.

The words that ended my fucking life with hers.

I'm so sorry.

I briefly close my eyes to push away the onslaught of memories—the look on her face, the way her legs gave out…

She should be standing here with me as we visit Mom's grave. She would've told me not to hate the man who acted as our father. She would've said she missed Mom and hugged me.

Since I was ten, I've known Alexander is a useless father. If I wanted my baby sister and me to have a good life after Mom, I needed to step up. So I did just that; I became her mother, father, brother, and best friend.

I became Ari's world, and she was mine.

Until she left me and joined Mom.

I lean over and stroke my fingers over the tombstone. At her funeral, I sat here for the entire night wondering where I had gone wrong.

Was I too protective? Was I not attentive enough? Was I too fucking stupid?

Then I realized, I hadn't done anything. Ari had told me she was sorry. She hadn't wanted to leave me, but she couldn't stay in this world.

A world in which Reina existed.

After that, I decided to leave, because I didn't want to be in such a world either. I didn't want to see her fucking breathing when my only family lay six feet under.

Alexander doesn't count. For me, he was only a sperm

donor, never a father. Writing checks made him a sponsor, not a parent.

Actually, he was a parent to Reina more than to his real children. She's his precious partner's daughter and a source of income. We were a fucking liability he had to spend his money on.

When I left for England, I promised I'd put everything behind me.

Back then, Reina knew exactly what I thought about her, and I wanted her to suffer until the day she dies. I wanted the guilt to eat her from the inside out, until she's old and gray and still living in Blackwood.

And she accepted her punishment. *Our* punishment.

But she broke the rules that night.

She wanted to escape.

Fuck *that*. Fuck my patience for seeing her decimated little by little.

I'm done watching, done trying to stay away.

Reina will pay, and she'll do it my way. She'll do it while hanging off the edge of a rooftop, bound and tied and begging for help that won't come.

"Her grave will be next to yours and mine, Ari."

My sister was my purpose in life. The day she died, I died with her.

The thing that rose from the ashes was a demon thirsty for blood.

Reina's blood.

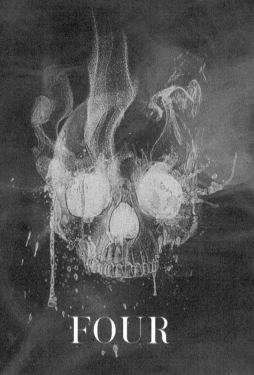

FOUR

Asher

The moment Alexander steps into the cemetery, I take my leave.

He gives me the stink eye and I'm tempted to fight him, but I'd never do that in front of Ari's grave.

I wonder if his assistant reminded him that today is the anniversary of his daughter's death. I wonder if he's only doing this for the appearance of it or if he actually remembers just how much Ari loved him despite his uselessness.

The drive home is similar to riding straight back to hell. Blackwood's buildings extend as far as the eye can see—all majestic, and so fucking empty like the people inside them.

In this town, people like Ari never fit in. The quiet nerds, the shy people who don't dress for fashion or socialize—those are the outcasts, the ones no one cares about or notices the absence of.

In this godforsaken town, people like Reina and me rule—popular and beautiful and fucking monstrous.

We were born to be at the top of the food chain while Ari was always destined to be at the very bottom where anyone could step on her.

Three years ago, I left and never looked back. The hypocrisy and…something else suffocated me. I had to stay the fuck away from Blackwood.

Until I didn't.

Until I returned like I'd never left.

It's funny how three years can seem too long and yet too short at the same time.

On the surface, nothing's changed. Blackwood is still filled with hollow souls and faceless people. Deep down, it's almost unrecognizable.

I park in front of the house and stride toward the entrance. No idea what the fuck I'm doing here. This is the last place I want to be on Ari's death anniversary.

This is where she first met Reina, and I smiled when they became friends.

Like a fucking idiot.

I loosen my tie; the thing restricts my breathing. My movements pause when the door to the pool house opens. Jason comes out first and hops over the step then offers his hand with a smile.

Pale soft fingers latch onto his, and my grip on the tie turns deadly.

I know who it is before she steps outside. Those fingers. That fucking hand.

All the pent-up energy that's been plaguing me since the morning translates into a red mist that covers my eyes and strangles my breathing. The need to cut off his hand and feed it to the dogs overwhelms me.

How fucking dare he touch what's mine?

How dare she fucking let him?

My murderous gaze flits from her to him. My demons whisper at me to go over, punch Jason in the goddamn face, and take back what's mine.

Reina is mine. Fucking mine.

And I'll screw the world so she'll remain that way.

What I have planned for her doesn't contradict that fact. Just because I gave her freedom doesn't mean she can parade around with another man as if she has every right to.

What were they doing in the pool house anyway?

I only stop my murderous plans when Jason waves at her and heads toward the small house he shares with Elizabeth. Reina barely acknowledges him as her feet carry her in my direction.

She doesn't lift her head so she can't see me watching the slight tremble in her full lips, the way her blond hair falls to her shoulder with abandonment. Her shorts ride up her pale thighs with every step she takes as if enticing me with what's beneath, with what I tasted last night.

The moment I had her, the moment I buried myself into her warmth and looked into her ocean blue eyes, I felt a strange energy.

It's like the ocean's pull when it's drowning you, or the sirens' song when they're luring you to nothingness.

Reina has that effect on people.

She lures then traps.

She manipulates then strikes.

She's the devil dressed as an angel.

For three years, that's what I believed, and I still do—in some way.

It's just that she came up with this fucking amnesia thing that keeps shuffling my cards. She keeps acting in sporadic ways that mess with my fucking head.

She's not supposed to get into my head, let alone mess with it.

My plan was simple: torture then kill her. Make her suffer then finish her miserable life.

Make her mine one final time then toss her aside.

Now the lines are blurring with every word out of her fucking mouth, with the way she got on her knees for me, the way she submitted to me, the way she opened her mouth and legs as if they've always belonged to me. They do.

She hasn't only done it with me. I've noticed the way she treats her cheerleaders, how she laughs and talks back, how she fucking smiles.

Reina doesn't smile.

She stopped smiling around her sixteenth birthday.

When she does, they're filled with contempt and malice. *Fake.*

Since the hospital, I've caught her smiling and laughing from the bottom of her heart more times than I can count.

I took pictures of those smiles while she wasn't watching and studied them later to see if she was putting on a front again.

She wasn't.

They were almost as genuine as when we were pre-teens.

She's not smiling now, though. Her shoulders strain with tension and her head appears lost elsewhere. She passes beside me without as much as a glance.

I doubt she even notices I'm there.

Her steps are heavy and slow as she takes the stairs, clutching the railings for balance.

I release the tie with a jerk.

Since waking up in the hospital, this is the first time Reina hasn't acknowledged my existence. She'd usually sense me a mile away and lock gazes with me with defiance and spikiness that makes my cock hard.

She'd light this thing inside me, a fire, an inkling, a fucking connection I thought I'd never feel to a human being again.

The Reina from today is different. She's so fucking similar to her old self.

But isn't that what I want? Old Reina is someone I can deal with, someone I can torture and kill. She'd deserve it. That's why I demanded she go back to her old ways.

Now that I'm getting what I wished for, I want to grip her by the throat and fuck that old bitch out of her.

Is the new Reina dead?

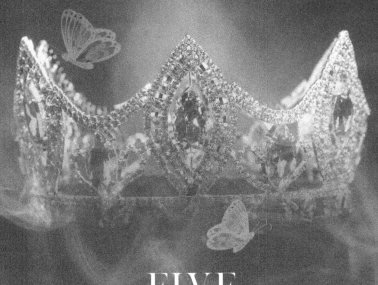

FIVE

Reina

I stay in my room for two days—or that's what I've determined based on counting the number of meals Izzy has brought me.

That gloomy cloud hovers over my head like imminent doom.

I fought it, you know—I tried to, anyway.

I tried not to let it occupy my thoughts, but at some point, it just did.

For the first time, I had no appetite for the food Izzy left in front of the door. I didn't even shower or change clothes. I didn't sleep or do anything.

For two days, I curled up under the covers in the dark and allowed those black thoughts to seep in.

They keep whispering and murmuring in hushed voices as if no one else should hear them. They're only meant for me, after all.

Why don't you just let go?

Why are you holding on to a life that means nothing to you?

No one would notice you're missing, you know.

No fucking one.

Tingles assault my nose and pressure builds behind my eyes, but I don't cry. It's like I can't. I don't have the right to.

I don't have the right to anything.

I've been resisting the cloud's whispers and murmurs, but why should I? What is there to resist?

My life is a clusterfuck, and although I have nothing to lose, I have nothing to gain either.

If I go against Asher, if I make him pay for what he did to me, what good would it bring?

Will I feel liberated at the end? Would I find a new purpose for life?

He knocked on my door yesterday. I didn't answer and he went away.

Good. I don't want to see his face again, not ever.

I don't want to think about how he played with my heart, body, and mind, how he allowed the gloomy cloud to sweep over me.

Or did he?

After all, the gloomy cloud is all in my head. I realize that, I do, but that doesn't mean I can resist it.

My armor is still unable to rebuild after the shocks I've received.

A knock on the door startles me from my numb state. I don't answer. If it's Izzy, she'll leave the plate in front of the door then return to take it back as it is.

"Reina."

The heart I thought was long dead pulses back to life at

that voice, the deep voice with slight huskiness, the voice that brought me happiness right before he shattered it and left me in the clutches of this gloomy cloud.

The doorknob rattles then snaps back into place due to the lock. "Open up."

Why? So he can call me a monster and dig the knife deeper? So I'll look at his face and realize he was never mine and I've been a fool all along?

No, thanks.

Besides, he's after my life. He won't stop until he drains the last breath out of me. A full-body shudder snakes under my skin at the thought.

"Open the fucking door or I will smash it to the ground." His voice loses all patience, pulsing with pent-up rage.

I have no doubt he'll break the thing if he chooses to.

Do I care? No.

He can do whatever he wants, but if he expects me to be the one who opens that door for him, he'll be disappointed. It won't be happening.

Villains shouldn't be allowed inside under any circumstances. I made that mistake once, and look where it lead me.

"Reina." He growls my name in that deep masculine way that still makes my toes curl.

When will he stop getting to me? Next week? Next month? How about next year?

"Hide while you can," he says before his presence disappears from in front of the door.

I don't know how I feel he's no longer there, but I just do.

He's gone. For now.

I throw the covers off. Somehow, his visit has raised my

body temperature and sweat has broken out on my brows and temples.

He has that effect, Asher. He gets under your skin, and before you know it, he's trapping you, tying you up on a roof, suffocating you, and planning to kill you.

God, this is so fucked up.

The room is dark and smells of my breaths and the residual scent of Asher on the sheets: sandalwood and citrus, warmth and coldness.

I didn't change the sheets we fucked on. I probably should've, but I couldn't be bothered.

With the thick curtains drawn over the window, I don't even know if it's night or day.

I retrieve my phone to check the time. I put it on airplane mode and haven't paid it attention since.

It's five in the evening.

As soon as I turn off airplane mode, my phone buzzes with endless messages, emails, and missed calls from the squad. Lucy and Naomi sent me shouty texts about where I've been.

I think about making up some sort of a lie. After all, that's exactly how my life has been in the past: a liar, a homewrecker, and everything in between.

Besides, I don't want to explain the state I'm in. I don't even recognize it myself.

I contemplate telling them I have the flu when an Instagram DM catches my attention.

Cloud003. He sent it two days ago, meaning the night after Jason took me to the pool house.

It's like he was checking up on me. My chest warms at the thought.

Jason did come by yesterday, but after a knock and no reply, he left.

I click on the message.

Cloud003: ...

What the hell? Just three dots?

I type before I even think about it.

Reina-Ellis: What the fuck is that supposed to mean?

The reply is immediate.

Cloud003: Alien language. Keep up, Ellis.

That draws a small smile from me.

Reina-Ellis: What do you want from me?

Cloud003: Aside from your pussy?

I roll my eyes.

Reina-Ellis: Yes, aside from that.

Cloud003: Everything you have to offer, my slut.

Reina-Ellis: How about my dark thoughts?

I don't know why the hell I mention that. I guess I need someone to vent to. Sure, I could've said it to Jason in person, but the semi-anonymity—from his side, not mine—gives me an inexplicable sense of courage.

Cloud003: The gloomy cloud?

My lips fall open as I stare at the words.

Reina-Ellis: How do you know about that?

Cloud003: I know everything about you.

Reina-Ellis: Are you like in my brain or something?

Cloud003: I wish. That way, I'd know everything firsthand.

Maybe I've told him about it in our encounters in the past. After all, Old Reina admitted to having feelings for him. Maybe that's why Jason came to check on me.

Reina-Ellis: It's painful. I can't move or drink or eat or do anything. The only movement in my brain is this signal urging me to open the window and jump, just jump and see how freeing that is.

My fingers hover over the phone as the dots appear and disappear, indicating he's typing.

No idea why I admitted that to him. I didn't even admit it to myself earlier. All of a sudden, I needed those thoughts out there.

They're in the world and I can't take them back.

Cloud003: You jump in cheerleading—why would you want to jump in another way?

I don't know what I expected as his reply, but that definitely wasn't it. For some reason, I thought he'd make fun of me since he's a bit of a jerk. Or maybe I wanted him to make fun of me so I wouldn't feel this freaked out about these thoughts.

I pause, thinking about my reply.

Reina-Ellis: It's a different type of jump.

Cloud003: Don't.

Reina-Ellis: Don't?

Cloud003: You're my slut, remember? You don't get to end your life.

Reina-Ellis: I told you I'm no longer your slut.

Cloud003: I never agreed to that.

Reina-Ellis: Doesn't mean you get to tell me what to do.

Cloud003: What do you look forward to when you wake up in the morning?

My fingers hover over the screen as I read his reply. I… never thought of that.

Reina-Ellis: Nothing.

Cloud003: That's the problem. You need a purpose.

Reina-Ellis: I don't have one.

Cloud003: Yes, you do—being my slut, remember?

Reina-Ellis: *rolls eyes*

Cloud003: Fine. Let's think of another purpose aside from that. How about cheerleading? Your friends? Your family?

No. They're fun, but they're not necessarily things I look forward to doing every day.

Then it hits me like nothing before and I type the word as fast as I can.

Reina-Ellis: Redemption.

Cloud003: Redemption?

Reina-Ellis: Yeah, ever since I realized what type of person I was in the past, I wake up every day thinking about ways to fix it.

That's why I've been feeling down. Since I learned my redemption hit a solid wall with Asher, I lost the purpose and the need to continue.

I lost the will to live.

He's the one I wanted to atone to the most, and when I realized nothing I do will work on him, I just pulled into myself and allowed the gloomy cloud in.

It takes several seconds for his reply to come through.

Cloud003: Why?

Reina-Ellis: What do you mean by why?

Cloud003: Why is redemption important to you?

Reina-Ellis: Because I'm not Old Reina anymore. I don't know what I am or where I'm going from here, but I know I don't enjoy hurting people. It's just not me.

Cloud003: What if those you hurt don't forgive you?

My broken heart continues dying a slow death at the reminder of Asher. He certainly would never forgive me. His perception of me is loud and clear.

Reina-Ellis: Then at least I tried.

An epiphany hits me.

I tried.

If I don't try, how will I know Asher won't forgive me? Maybe I can change his perception or prove him wrong.

Old or New Reina would never hurt someone they considered a friend. It just doesn't work that way in my brain.

I never hurt Bree in the past and she's a bitch, so that should mean something.

A knock sounds on the door and I startle, nearly dropping the phone.

"Open up, Rei!" Naomi's voice hollers from outside. "I brought my tools. I can pick this lock."

"Stop it, Nao." Lucy's soft voice reprimands her before she addresses me. "Are you okay, Captain? Do you need anything? I just want you to know we're here for you, okay? Come out whenever you're ready."

"Yeah, campus is so boring without you or whatever," Naomi grumbles.

My insides expand at her words, and a full-body shudder takes over me.

Did you hear that, dark thoughts?

They care.

My feet move of their own volition as I stumble from the bed and nearly fall as the sheet wraps around my legs. I kick it off and approach the door like a scared kitten.

The click is loud in the silent room as I open the door, just the slightest bit, enough for my head to peek out. The light from the hallway blinds me and I squint, trying to adjust.

Naomi and Lucy stand there, both carrying their school bags.

"Hi," I whisper in a hoarse voice that doesn't resemble my own.

I must look like shit. My makeup must be smeared, my hair is in complete disarray, and my clothes are rumpled.

If they notice that, they don't comment. Lucy grins, her cheeks moving with the motion. Naomi straight-out kicks the door open and barges inside like it's her house.

"Chop-chop!" She snaps her fingers. "You need to shower stat, and we're getting out of this torture chamber."

"I'm so glad you opened up for us, Rei." Lucy engulfs me in a hug, and I fight the urge to sob as I wrap my arms around her.

I didn't know how much I needed their company, their presence, until this moment.

From now on, I won't allow that cloud to catch me all alone. It'll just swallow me alive and release a corpse.

Naomi pushes me toward the bathroom, declaring that I'm a grown-ass adult who should shower on her own.

I grin as she huffs and helps me by fumbling through my clothes to find me something to wear.

"Where are we going?" I ask as I come out of the shower with a towel wrapped around me and another around my hair.

Lucy is searching through the makeup as Naomi throws me a camisole and dark jeans. "Anywhere downtown."

"Not The Grill," Lucy says.

"What's that?" I ask as I dry my hair.

"A restaurant." Lucy takes the hair towel away. "Nao hates it."

"I don't *hate* it." She throws her hands in the air. "Actually, let's go there."

Lucy bites her lower lip. "Are you sure? Sebastian will be there."

"Fuck that asshole," she grumbles.

"Sideways," I add as I pull my hair up in a chignon. "Do you really hate him?"

Naomi's eyes nearly bug out. "Is that a trick question?"

"I thought...forget about it."

"No, what? Say it."

"I don't know. I thought there was something between you two. You act tough, but well, you watch him."

"I do not."

"Uh-huh." I grab the camisole and pull it over my head.

Naomi's expression turns to one of pure contempt. "Like you watch Asher?"

My chest squeezes and the good mood I've been in since they appeared nearly disappears. "This isn't about him."

"Yeah, right." Naomi flips her hair.

"We're just an illusion, like Lucy said." I flop in front of the mirror and stare at my eyes. They're becoming lifeless, like the somber depths of an ocean.

"That was before." Lucy clutches my shoulders from behind, looking at me through the mirror. "You guys are different now. You make me want to film your life."

"No, we're not."

"Uh-huh." Naomi throws the pants at my head and Lucy catches them. "Is that why he called us and asked us to check on you?"

My eyes widen as I face them. "He…he did that?"

Lucy's smile is soft and dreamy. "He sounded worried, too. I need an Asher in my life."

This can't be true.

Wait—is this another one of his games?

If he wants me dead, why would he worry about me?

It doesn't make any sense.

SIX

Reina

The following day, I go back to school.

I try to keep to myself and not talk to anyone except Naomi and Lucy. I can't take any jabs at my person while I'm still trying to push that gloomy cloud away.

It's clingy, you know.

Like super glue, it won't go the fuck away no matter how much I shake it off. It has less to do with my state of mind and more with how the fuck I'm supposed to carry on with my life after what I uncovered.

That doesn't mean I cower away from the snide remarks or the envious looks I keep getting from everyone around campus. Apparently, the locker room incident has been circulating around that shady Instagram account, blackwood-black-book. The fact that I disappeared two days afterward is one more reason for everyone to roast me, talk behind my back, and whisper at my face.

Blackwood College is full of fucking hypocrites. But then again, Old Reina gave them all the reasons to put her on a high pedestal. What she didn't know is that no matter how high you rise, one day you'll fall. The higher the position, the louder the crash.

Naomi, Lucy, and I go into the gym for practice. We have to try our routine a few more times before the game on Friday.

Lucy has been joking about some show, and my heart warms at how she tries to cheer me up and distract me from the venomous tongues following me everywhere.

As soon as we're inside, Bree stops mid-sentence in her conversation with Prescott. Both of them watch me with mouths agape.

"Captain?" she squeaks. "What are you doing here?"

Everyone else pauses mid-workout, watching us closely.

I sigh. "What does it look like I'm doing, Bree? I'm here for practice."

"Uh—no," she snaps. "You're the talk of everyone on campus, and not in a good way. The squad doesn't need that type of attention."

My gaze strays to the others. The boys lower their heads, some of them kicking imaginary rocks. The girls remain frozen, as if they'd rather not be here.

"She's still the captain," Naomi snaps back.

"A captain wouldn't bring that type of attention." Bree points a finger at Naomi. "And you of all people need to shut your trap. You don't practice like us. You don't diet like us. You shouldn't even be with us."

Naomi lunges in her direction, but I place a hand on her arm, stopping her in her tracks.

"You're not the one who decides who deserves to be on the

squad." I cross my arms over my chest and square my shoulders. "Are you, Bree?"

"Maybe I should be."

A few gasps sound from the other girls.

Prescott's eyes widen as he grabs her by the arm. "Bree."

She shakes him off and strides in my direction so we're standing toe to toe. "You don't deserve to be captain, Rei. Admit it."

Although I don't see the change, I feel it. My face must be becoming void of all emotions. My heartbeat slows down as if I'm not feeling anymore. My nails dig into the flesh of my arms as I glare down at Bree. When I speak, my tone is flat and non-negotiable. "Know your place before I put you back in it."

"I'm not scared of you anymore, Reina." She laughs, the squeaky sound bouncing off the walls. "Who would want to follow a captain who's constantly attacked and becoming the laughing stock on campus? Not me."

"Take a hike then," I say.

"How about *you* do that?" She points a finger at my shoulder. "We're removing you from the captain position."

I stare at the girls. "Who's removing me from the captain position?"

Almost everyone bows their heads.

"Don't be scared." Bree faces them. "Everyone who wants to remove Reina Ellis from the captain, raise your hand."

"Yes, raise your hand." My voice is still neutral. "But before you do, know this. Bree never cared about the squad or winning state. She already has a contract lined up for a dance institute and she wants the captain position to add it to her resume, not to help you achieve your dreams. Bree will keep calling you fat pigs even if you die of hunger. She'll always put the prettiest girls in the back because they threaten her. She'll always dye her hair the same color as mine and try to dress like me and act like me and steal my things, but guess what, Bree." I glare down at her flushed cheeks, my tone turning slow and stone-cold. "You'll *never* be me."

Her face nearly becomes crimson. "You fuck—"

"Watch your fucking mouth when you're talking to your captain," I cut her off.

Naomi told me about Bree's contract as soon as she decided she'd be allies with me. I knew my former best friend would pull this shit one day, and I wasn't going to leave the squad at her mercy.

Cheerleading might not be my goal in life, but this is my final year and I'll finish it with a hurrah. I'll make their dreams come true before I step down willingly.

No one will force me to leave like Bree is trying to.

"Go ahead." I face the squad. "Vote. Anyone want me out?"

No one raises their hand.

"You promised." Bree shrieks, but no one is giving her their attention. "Prescott!"

He just averts his gaze to the other boys.

"It's settled then." I release my nails from my flesh. "As I said, take a fucking hike, Bree."

Her groan is nearly animalistic as she pushes past me toward the locker room.

"That's what happens when you use others as stepping stones, *Bee!*" Naomi shouts after her.

Everyone else continues watching me as if I'll kick them out like I just did Bree.

"Go on." I motion around. "Continue what you were doing. Winning state doesn't happen by standing around."

"Yes, Captain!" Like a hive of bees, everyone returns to warming up or practicing throws. Naomi and Lucy grin at me before joining the rest.

"Prescott," I call as he heads over to the boys.

He winces before turning around and facing me. I point at a secluded corner, and he joins me without so much as one word of protest. Once we're out of earshot, I watch him closely. His shoulders are drooping underneath the male cheerleading uniform and he's averting his gaze.

Prescott is the male co-captain, and if I'm going to make things work, I need to see eye to eye with him while still keeping my authority.

He hasn't hidden the fact that he's on Bree's side since I returned, and I need to see the end of that.

"What did I do to you before?" I don't beat around the bush.

"C-Captain?" He seems taken aback, as if he didn't expect that question.

"I obviously hurt you in some way."

He hesitates.

"Tell me, Prescott." I soften my tone. "If we're going to lead this team, we have to make our relationship work. Help me out here."

He swallows. "This...this is the first time you've ever asked me to help you."

"It won't be the last. A captain needs trusted leaders. Now, tell me."

"It was nothing, really."

"Let me be the judge of that."

He interlinks his fingers then releases them. "Last year, you said you'd hook me up with Lucy then, well, you told me I don't deserve her and to fuck off. You threatened that if I approached Lucy in any way, you'd cause problems for my parents—they work for your dad's company."

I pause. For some reason, I don't think I would've made that threat without anything to back it up. Perhaps I cared for Lucy and I thought Prescott really didn't deserve her.

As much as I loathe Old Reina, she had reasons for acting the way she did. She wasn't stupid.

She was just emotionless—on the surface. No idea how she coped with things inside.

Maybe that's why I lost my memories and came back with this new version of me—a version that has made more peace with her emotions and shows them on the outside.

"What happened between when I promised you and when I told you to forget it?"

He lifts a shoulder. "Nothing."

"Think carefully. Something must've happened."

"I guess you caught me fooling around with a sophomore— but it was just a kiss and we were drunk and she looked so much like Lucy. Fuck. You think it was because of that?"

If I thought Prescott wasn't serious about Lucy, I would've definitely offed him. "Could be. Were you also close to Bree?"

"A little. I mean, you were best friends with her."

Or maybe I pretended to be best friends with her for other reasons.

Old Reina had an interesting brain. It'll take me some time to get into it, but I'll eventually figure out her thought process.

"Are you going to be on my side or do I have to treat you as an enemy?" I ask him.

"I want what's best for the squad."

"Wonderful. And Prescott?"

"Yeah?"

"Do you have a girlfriend?"

He lowers his eyes. "No."

"If I deem you worthy and if Lucy agrees, I'll lift the ban."

His expression lights up as he stares between me and Lucy, who's struggling to have Naomi hold her up. "Is this another game?"

"No games." I pat his shoulder. "Don't disappoint me."

After practice, I shower and walk out with Lucy and Naomi. They keep following me around. Even though they're not voicing it, I know they won't leave me alone for fear I'll be attacked again.

If I didn't know who attacked me, I might be scared as well. I might look over my shoulder and search for those green eyes that were eating away at my soul.

Now, I have a different type of plan, one they don't need to know about. If they did, they'd tell me not to do it.

Since I woke up at the hospital, I haven't been as sure about anything as I am about this.

My phone vibrates. My lips pull into a smile as the name pops up in my notifications.

Cloud003: Any gloomy clouds today?

My heart flutters with tiny bursts of happiness. He remembers. I don't know why I feel so touched that he does.

Reina-Ellis: I'm trying to get rid of it.

Cloud003: How's that working for you?

Reina-Ellis: Not so well.

Cloud003: I'm sure you'll make it. You're a fighter.

I bite my lower lip.

A fighter.

Why does that single word fill me with so much energy? It buzzes under my skin, demanding I shout it.

I'm a fighter. A survivor.

Reina-Ellis: How do you know that?

Cloud003: I just do.

I smile.

Cloud003: After all, you're my slut, remember?

And he had to ruin it.

Jerk.

I type that word and send it over. He replies with a winking emoji. For some reason, it feels so intimate, like maybe he's winked at me that way in real life. Maybe our connection was more than sex after all.

Despite Reina's snobbish attitude, she reached out to him and asked to meet him, and I know for certain Old Reina didn't put herself out there without a reason.

Did I know it was Jason back then? Honestly, with Reina's level of secretive conniving, it could have gone either way.

"Aren't you coming?" Lucy motions at her MINI Cooper.

"I have to meet Alex." I cock my head toward a taxi. "I already called my ride."

"Text us if you can hang out later." Naomi opens the passenger door.

"I will." I wave at them, keeping a smile plastered on my face until they disappear from view.

I lied.

I'm not meeting with Alex, but I had to say that so they wouldn't question me.

If they knew where I'm going, they would either stop me or insist they come along. It will only work if I go there alone like I did before.

If I want to recover my memories, I need to go back to where it all started.

I slide into the back seat and tell the driver, "Blackwood Forest."

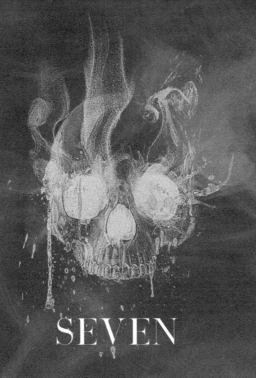

SEVEN

Asher

I remain behind as Reina walks with her two friends. Lucy and Naomi are the ones who brought her out of her room yesterday and the ones she likes to spend most of her time with.

In the past, she would've been all over Brianna's plastic personality—another thing that's changed about Reina.

Owen told me earlier about some sort of war between Reina and Brianna over the captain position and how Reina kicked her supposed best friend off the team.

It sounds so much like Old Reina, and yet, it isn't. I can nearly taste the tangible change in her.

The way she talks, walks, and looks is the same, but the attitude isn't.

The constant talking back isn't.

The fucking smile certainly isn't.

That day when she brushed past me without a glance, I felt something I never thought I would feel again.

Grief.

I was grieving the new Reina, thinking she'd completely disappeared.

The moment she came out of her room with her friends, I released a breath. Then I got fucking angry at myself for letting her crawl under my skin this way.

She's been doing it subtly, but it's there. Every time I wake up, she's the first person who comes to mind.

And to my fucking dismay, they're not thoughts about the best way to destroy her. No. They're thoughts about *her*.

Her state of mind. What does she want? Where is she going? Who is she thinking about?

If I let my brain loose, it'll be the reason for my downfall, so I fill it with different thoughts.

Reina is mine to rule and own.

That's the only reason I'm letting her get away with occupying my thoughts.

At the parking lot, Reina waves at her friends. Her little leather skirt barely reaches the middle of her thighs. The black color contrasts with her skin, making it look like the most delectable meal waiting to be served. Her top falls over one shoulder, revealing the curve of her neck as she pushes her blond strands to one side.

If temptation had a name, it'd be Reina.

Her hips sway gently as she turns around, hips that are made for my fucking hands as I grab them and slam into her warmth.

My cock twitches and I groan, readjusting my sunglasses. It's been less than a week since I had her all to myself.

In my dick's memory, that's a long fucking time.

It wouldn't feel this desperate if I hadn't had her, if I'd kept to my rules and made my cock wait.

Now that I've had a taste, I want her hands, mouth, and pussy for myself.

I want all of her.

My fantasies come to a screeching halt when I make out the determined expression on her face, the darkening of her eyes and the closing off of her features.

Old Reina's traits.

She's out for trouble.

She's out to destroy someone's life.

Her expression disappears as she enters the taxi. I retrieve my keys and stride to my car.

Only one way to find out her plans.

EIGHT

Reina

I stand in the middle of the burned cottage in the forest.

The walls are black from the remains of the fire. The sun slips in through the cracks between the stones and the ceiling that's half gone.

Despite the rays of sunshine, a cold gust of wind whirls around me as if trying to kick me out. It still smells of smoke and a bit of pine, like the trees standing tall around here. Some yellow police tape surrounds the area, but no one guards it.

If they suspect there's been a murder, how could they deem it good to go? After all, Detective Daniels seems hell-bent on catching the perpetrator.

In the small space, I stand with my back to the half-burned door. My chest has been clenching since the moment I paid the cabbie and told him he was good to go.

This is where the police found human remains and

my bracelet. It's close to where I was found afterward, so I must've been here.

I must've been at the crime scene.

Human remains.

A shudder races down my spine at the thought. What could I have been doing with the person whose remains they found?

Since Lucy's father is the police deputy commissioner, I've been asking her if she's heard anything.

Apparently, they're all keeping quiet about it, but from what she learned by eavesdropping, the police still don't have a body or enough remains to create a profile.

I've been praying the person is only badly injured and not dead.

Despite my tough talk, I can't live with the fact that I witnessed someone's murder and did nothing about it—or worse, participated in it.

With heavy feet, I walk to a stone bench in the corner. For some reason, it seems familiar.

Way too familiar.

I retrieve a napkin and wipe the dust and soot from the surface then sit down. It feels right to sit here.

So, *so* right.

My fingers trail over the back of the bench, my brows furrowing. It's right to be here, but there's something wrong.

Or rather, something missing.

My eyes widen.

It's not something. It's *someone.*

I inhale the pine scent coming from outside as the memory hits me like sparkling fireworks on the Fourth of July.

Night of the incident

I sit on the bench, my eyes filled with tears. All the way here, I've been hardly holding on.

Now that she's sitting right in front of me, it's nearly impossible to stop the onslaught of emotions.

Her hair is a bit shorter than mine and she's got it up in a ponytail. She has the same deep blue eyes, the same full lips with the teardrop at the upper lip, the same tiny nose that fits the shape of her face.

Reina.

She's finally here. We finally found our way back to each other after nine years.

She stares at the engagement ring on her finger. It glints under the cottage's soft light as she grins.

I cross my arms over my chest. "Are you here for me or for that engagement ring?"

"The ring. Definitely the ring."

I huff. "Whatever."

"You're just being jealous." Reina hits my shoulder with hers. "It's not my fault I got all the looks."

"Oh, *puh-leeze*." I flip my hair. "Are you even looking at me?"

"Yeah." Her grin is a little sad this time. "I see me."

"I see me, too. Rei…" I grab her hands in mine. "I'm going to make things right for the both of us. I'm making that promise come true. You saved me. It's time I save you."

She shakes her head, expression calm and wise. "I don't want you involved. Dad was, and we both know where that led him. I won't lose you, too, Rai."

I jerk up, running a hand through my hair as I pace the

length of the cottage. "You can't expect me to sit and do nothing. Dad would've understood."

"Rai." She stands up and slowly approaches me, as if she's afraid of setting me off. "Listen to me. Dad knew why I had to do this. Why do you think he kept it a secret? Besides, I have someone who'll help me, but you have nothing, okay? You don't know these people as much as I do. They'll murder you and bury your remains at a new construction site. They're dangerous people."

"Are you listening to yourself?" Tears well in my eyes. "If they're dangerous, how do you expect me to leave you in their clutches and carry on as if nothing happened?"

"You forget a little trick, sis." She grins, rubbing her nose with her index finger like she used to do when we were children. "I've been studying them for years. I can handle them."

"Reina..." My voice breaks. "I just can't watch you slip through my fingers again. I can't."

"I won't slip away." She rubs her hand on my arm in a soothing gesture. "We're one, after all. You'll feel me even if we're apart. Do you remember those days with Mom?"

I snort. How could I not remember? When we were twelve, Reina and I met for the first time. Even though we had people after us and we had to sleep at different hotels and hostels every night, those months were the happiest times of my life.

I had a mother and a sister.

Then they were both taken away from me.

We were separated for nine years. For most of those nine years, I thought Reina was dead. I searched for her all around and even made deals with a lot of 'criminals'.

Finally, I scored the right people and she came in contact.

The day I received an invitation from her to come to this place was probably the happiest day of my life.

Just when I was starting to give up, she showed me a sign.

She came back for me like she'd promised back then.

I'm older, you know, she'd scolded. *I'll be the one who finds you.*

She kept her promise.

She's here.

But not for long.

"Mom was smart," Reina continues, "but she wasn't that smart, Rai. It's useless to run away in a pack. They would've always found us. Diversion, remember?"

"What if I don't want to? What if I want to run away with you?"

Her face falls. "Then it'll be like Mom all over again."

"I *hate* this."

"I do too." She ruffles my hair. "But I'm coming back. You won't get rid of me."

"Promise?"

"Promise, Rai."

Present

I'm pushed back to the now with a crippling force.

I gasp for air as if I've been drowning underwater.

Rai.

Oh my God. My name is not Reina—it's Rai.

Reina was the other one, the one who told me she'd come back, the one who stopped me from going with her.

I jump to my wobbly feet and walk to the spot where both of us stood that night. She hugged me, and we made a promise.

We talked and then...what?

I stare at the black walls, at the cracks in them.

We found human remains.

The detective's words bounce in my head like an atomic bomb.

No, no, no.

Fuck no.

It's not Reina. They didn't find Reina's remains. They couldn't have.

I pace the length of the cottage, back and forth, back and forth like a trapped animal. They took my sister away from me.

After I finally found her, they fucking took her away.

But who are they?

Reina and I were talking just fine that night. We were planning things and then...what? What the fuck happened after that?

I rack my brain for answers, but nothing comes out.

It's blank in there. Or maybe it's too jumbled up for anything to be clear.

Reina.

I had a twin. No, *have*. I refuse to believe she's not here anymore. We made a fucking promise.

But if she were alive, wouldn't she have found me by now? Wouldn't she have stepped up?

No, no. She can't be dead. I can't lose her like I lost Mom.

Like I lost Mom.

Mom.

Mom...?

The jolt hits me like a bolt. I stagger backward and fall on the damp floor. My limbs spasm and my ears ring.

Shouting echoes in my head like a distant memory, damnation—something I don't want to remember.

I cover my ears with sweaty fingers, unable to take it anymore.

Nine years ago

"Take your sister and run, Rai! Run!!" Mom's voice echoes in my head like the pounding of a bell.

The shuffling of feet comes close to us. They pound on the door. They're coming for us.

"Run!" she screams at us. "Don't look back. Run!"

We do.

My hand clasps Reina's as we sprint through the back door. The streets are dark and smell of puke, so much puke.

Reina covers her nose with the sleeve of her thin sweater and motions at me to do the same.

It only reduces the smell a little.

It's atrocious, the scent. I wish I could say I got used to it after sleeping in dirty places, but I didn't. This pungent sensory assault never gets normal.

"She's not here!" Mom yells. I want to turn around, but Reina shakes her head.

There's screaming, shouting, and then something hits the floor behind us, but we don't turn around.

We run.

We just run.

Mom screams, her voice echoing in the air like a bomb.

"Here, Boss!" someone shouts closer to us.

"Darn it!" Reina pulls me behind a container by the sleeve.

"Don't touch her!" Mom shrieks, but she's gurgling on something like her mouth is full of water. "Don't you dare or Papa will—"

A pop silences Mom. She's no longer shrieking or talking. She's no longer…there.

My widened eyes meet Reina's. I start to run back, to go see Mom, but my sister shakes her head, tears welling in her eyes. "Mom said to never look back."

"But—"

Reina stifles my words as footsteps approach us.

"I saw her. She's here." The gruff voice makes goosebumps rise on my arms.

"Get her. Boss won't accept any mistakes."

Reina's clutch on my arm turns steel-like. She leans in, her face like Mom's when she's about to say something bad.

I shake my head frantically before she even speaks. "No."

"Shh." She places a trembling finger on my lips, shushing me and glancing behind her as the thundering footsteps get closer. "You'll be okay, Rai."

I continue shaking my head, unable to stop. My fingers strangle the bracelet Mom gave me for my birthday. It's a bit big and I have to roll it twice, but it's Mom's most precious gift. She said she got it from her own mother, and now, she was giving it to me.

"They're after Mom's daughter," Reina says. "I don't think they know about me. They only know about you."

"No."

"I lived well with Daddy, Rai." Tears glisten down her cheeks. "We didn't have to run like you and Mom. We didn't have to eat leftovers or sleep on the streets. I want you to have that. I want you to have my life."

"Reina..." I choke.

"You're Reina now. I'll be Rai."

"No...no..." I hold on to her hand, shaking and whispering my denials like a prayer.

She caresses my hair. "I love you, little sis. I'll find you."

"No, Rei."

"You're Rei," she whispers. "It's our secret. I'll live as you and you'll live as me." Her bottom lip trembles. "Take care of Daddy. Tell him you love him every day on my behalf." I open my mouth to say something, but she pushes me. "Now, run. Don't look back. Never look back."

Footsteps approach as I hold on to her hand.

"Run!" she hisses.

My feet kick into gear as I stumble in the opposite direction.

"I'm here!" Reina's voice echoes behind me, but I follow her instructions and don't look back.

Never look back.

"Boss! The girl is here!" yells a thickly accented voice.

I round the corner and run until my legs nearly give out, until my breathing stutters. Snot and tears cover my face, but I don't stop running. I run and run until I think I'll collapse and they'll catch me.

Don't look back.

Never look back.

I don't know how long I run. I don't know how far my legs carry me. Then, I stumble and fall.

Someone in a uniform approaches me. I shrink into the pole, breathing harshly and hugging my knees to my chest.

The tears won't stop. Mom and Reina's voices won't leave my head.

They just won't.

Murmurs. Screams. Hisses.

They're all there, in my head.

"Are you okay, kid?" The uniformed man crouches in front of me. He has a red beard and tattoos down his arms.

He looks like the pigs who've chased Mom and me all our lives.

I shrink further into the pole, clutching my bracelet tight.

"Kid? Have you lost your way home?"

He doesn't have an accent like those guys, but he could be one of them.

Don't trust anyone. The world is out to get you, Rai, Mom used to tell me.

"Wait." He reaches into his pocket and retrieves a picture then studies it and me intently. "You're that mogul's missing daughter." He retrieves a device from his pocket and says a number then something about finding the missing child. "What's your name?" he asks me. "Do you remember your name and where you came from?"

Rai Sokolov. Daughter of Mia Sokolov. I've been on the run since the day I was born, homeschooled my entire life, and had no friends until Mom brought my long-lost twin sister to meet me a month ago.

Then, they were both taken away.

My mom and my sister.

The only one I have left is my dad. If I want to be with him, I have to forget my life and embrace another one.

A tear falls down my cheek as I whisper, "Reina. My name is Reina Ellis."

NINE

Asher

Reina has returned to the forest.

What the fuck is she doing here?

My shoulders are about to fucking snap with tension as I trail through the tall trees, pushing away the low branches.

Does she have a death wish? Those who attacked her that day could be lurking here, waiting for her return.

It was fucking ugly, and that says something considering I hated her at the time.

Hated her? Past tense?

I still fucking do.

My plan is in place. It's chipped and ragged around the edges, but it's still the same.

Then what the hell are you doing here?

I briefly close my eyes, eradicating that voice.

I only came because she doesn't get to die by someone else's hand. Her life is mine, fucking *mine*, and she has no right to end it without permission.

That's it.

That's *all*.

My steps turn wider and harder as I cut through the distance. Dry leaves crunch under my shoes, and the smell of the forest is nearly asphyxiating.

The sun has begun its descent, casting a somber hue on the trees.

Darkness never scared me before. It was a place to take refuge in. Darkness is where the monsters become invisible, and I've long since converted to the other side.

I've long since given up on what people consider normal. My life is anything but.

My life has been submerged in darkness since Ari's death, and I've inflicted it on the world—or rather, on *her*.

Reina.

She's the subject of my darkness now, and nothing will save her from the things my wired brain is planning.

Nothing will save her from me.

She might be a monster, but there are degrees in those. Her level would never reach mine. Reina was bound to lose before we even got started.

I would pity her if she hadn't already killed that part of me.

If she hadn't pushed her off the edge and let her head shatter to pieces.

The image of Ari's smashed face and her limbs lolling in awkward positions still haunts my nightmares.

Her ghost still visits me in the darkness, asking me to let her soul rest in peace.

This isn't revenge; this is fucking justice.

Which Reina has never been served in her life.

There's no doubt in my mind she headed to that cottage, so I don't bother with searching the forest and stride straight there.

As the trees and the earthly ground blur in my vision, I can't help recalling that night.

The night Reina could've been gone once and for all.

The night of the accident

Reina leaves early.

She never leaves her precious squad and cheerleading buddies first. Being a perfectionist who always makes sure everyone does their tasks, she's usually the last to go home.

The break in pattern and her suspicious behavior can only mean one thing.

She's running away and leaving Blackwood.

Fuck *no.*

I trail her to the forest, which happens to be at the edge of town. She's definitely leaving.

Well, she has a surprise waiting.

I park my car at the front and continue on foot.

Black is the only color in the forest. It's a moonless night without stars in sight.

The deep silence stakes its claim, refusing to budge. I retrieve my phone and turn on the flashlight.

Ideally, I don't want her to know I'm onto her until I'm at her face. I want to see her expression falter a little, her eyes widening the slightest bit, before she seals herself in.

That's about the only time I get to see a reaction in her

robotic face. Reina hides her emotions so fucking well, and it made me a motherfucking idiot during high school.

I made it a habit to stand outside her house, just to see her laugh with her father.

I even took a picture as proof that she does smile and laugh—just not with me.

Shaking my head, I forge ahead. Thankfully, that idiot and his irrational fixation on Reina died with Ari.

Now there's this *thing*, one made for one purpose only: to make her pay for killing my sister and me.

A long shriek comes from my right.

My feet freeze to a halt, and then they're running toward the sound of their own volition.

Reina.

That's Reina's voice.

What the fuck did she get herself into this time?

I focus in case she shrieks again, but there's no sound.

Fuck.

She better not be dead.

My athletic body kicks into gear as I cut the distance in record time. I might have stopped playing football three years ago, but I never quit running or working out.

It's the only thing that clears my mind and chases away the damn black thoughts swirling in my head 24-7.

The smell of smoke assaults my nostrils as fire erupts in the middle of the forest.

Near the flames, two bodies come into view from between the trees. I hide behind a trunk and kill my flashlight.

The man is wearing a suit, appearing buff and big, but his face is shadowed and turned away as he drags someone on the ground by the hem of her T-shirt.

Reina.

He's dragging an unconscious Reina. From the slight view I can get, I make out her battered face and how her lifeless legs slide on the filthy ground.

My muscles turn tight as my fists clench by my sides. How fucking dare he touch her?

I'm about to move when another man emerges from behind the cottage, wiping his hands on his black hoodie. "I got the other one, Boss." He motions at Reina. "What are we going to do about that one?"

"Use her as bait. There'll be only one Pakhan."

Russian accents. Are they the mafia?

What do they have to do with Reina?

This could be about Gareth Ellis' relationship with the mafia, but they shouldn't come after his daughter.

Doesn't matter. I have a fraction of a second before they take Reina away to God knows fucking where.

Reina's life is mine.

Fucking *mine*.

No one gets to take her away from me.

I retrieve my phone and search for sounds then hit play on the loudest volume. The sound of sirens erupts in the otherwise calm forest. It's far away at the beginning but keeps getting closer as the seconds tick on.

Both men freeze.

"*Blyad!*" one of them yells. "What are they doing here?"

"What are we going to do, Boss?" the other man asks.

"We'll come back for her. We have what we need." He kicks Reina away and a whimper spills from her lips.

My fist tightens with the need to snap his fucking neck.

Both of them run around the burned cottage, and Reina

remains there, unmoving. I hear the sound of car tires crunching in the distance, indicating that they've left.

I jog to Reina and crouch in front of her, keeping the siren audio working.

She's on her stomach, face down. The fire from the cottage in the distance lights the deep blue bruises on her face and arms. Her blond strands fall on her face, camouflaging her swollen eye and cut lip.

Those motherfuckers.

I stroke the hair off her eye and she whimpers in pain.

Pulling my hand back, I search in her pocket and retrieve her phone. Sure, I could've used mine, but I don't want her to know I saved her.

I'm not her savior. I'm her worst nightmare.

I put the phone to my ear, and a woman picks up immediately.

"911, what's your emergency?"

"A girl has been attacked in the forest at the edge of Blackwood. She's unconscious but still breathing. Trace her GPS."

"Who are you, sir?"

I stand up, looking down at her. "A hunter."

I cut off the call and remain by her side until actual sirens come to the site.

That's when I retreat to the shadows and disappear.

But she'll find me in her hospital room as soon as she wakes up, and she'll fucking tell me why she was escaping.

Present

I stop in front of the cottage. The signs of the fire that ate it a few weeks ago are still visible through the blackened walls and the police tape.

Human remains.

The other one.

The police and those men's words still echo in my head. Reina is in too deep if she's involved with the bratva.

And they were from the bratva. Alex thinks so, too; I confirmed it when I heard his conversation with his adviser the other day.

He just doesn't want to take any steps as long as Reina remains untouched and under his care.

The question is, what the fuck is she doing here knowing exactly the threat to her life? Alex made sure to warn her. I heard him countless times.

Stay in crowded places, Reina.

If you remember anything, let me know first, Reina.

I'm going to get you security, Reina.

Of course, she refused the latter, brushing him off with a smile—a fake one at that.

She's become so fucking stubborn, it's maddening.

I release a breath as I walk up. She's been avoiding me these last couple of days, but fuck that.

Me being a part of her life is a non-negotiable fact.

Even when I was in England for the past three years, I was always an undividable part of her life.

I lurked under her skin and breathed down her neck.

She's been doing the same, but fuck it.

I stop at the threshold of the cottage. It's dark and humid inside, still smelling of the soot and the smoke from that day.

Human remains, they said, and they think Reina did it— at least that detective does.

I talked to him after the last time he visited us. I could see the malice in his eyes as he spoke about my 'fiancée' as a criminal and said I should have her confess her crimes.

It took all my self-restraint not to bash his head against the hood of his car and tell him, in no uncertain terms, that if he threatens her again, I will gut his intestines out.

Reina didn't do it.

It's funny how I believe it with every fiber of my being even though I didn't witness what happened.

The bratva is behind all of this, but I can't say anything because I have no evidence, no names, not even clear descriptions of the men I saw that night.

If I gave an unintelligible statement, it'd only make the mafia target me—and Reina.

For some reason, I think they've kept away because they figured she lost her memories and said nothing about them to the police.

If she does remember, it'll be a direct threat to her life.

Still, she needs to get herself off of Detective Daniels' radar.

He doesn't know her as much as I do, so he has no idea she absolutely doesn't have what it takes to end a life. She only does it from afar, like with Ari.

Ending a life takes something more than courage and determination. It takes a black heart and a desolate soul.

To my fucking dismay, the new Reina doesn't have that.

I halt at the entrance as I turn on the flashlight. Reina lies in a fetal position on the ground, eyes closed and face camouflaged by her hair.

My breathing stops as I wait for the rise and fall of her shoulder—for evidence that she's alive.

When it does move, my feet run of their own volition, like that day when all I thought about was her safety.

Once again, that's all I think about.

I try to tell my pulse to stay the fuck down, but it's not listening to me. I direct the light at her face as I crouch in front of her.

"Reina?" My movements are slow as I push a strand of blond hair off her face.

Her brows are furrowed together, mouth twisting in agony. Her eyes are shut so tight, it appears painful.

Something snaps in my chest, a feeling I never wanted to experience after those years in high school.

When I thought she was the only one for me.

"Open your fucking eyes, Reina."

She mumbles something under her breath. I lean over to hear her, but it's not making sense. She's speaking in a foreign language.

Is that Russian?

"R-Rai...Rai..."

Who the fuck is Rai?

Reina and her endless secrets just keep mounting over the years.

I place an arm under her pale, bare thighs and the other around her back to carry her in my arms.

She fits so perfectly, like she was made for my hands. She was made for *me*.

I watch the furrowing of her brows as her head drops against my chest. She looks so fragile right now, so soft, like the girl I saw for the first time after she disappeared when we were twelve. It was the first time I decided I liked that girl, the first time I thought about kissing a girl.

She was Gareth's only daughter, so I'd met her before, but I had never felt the need to come closer to her like when she returned. There was something changed about her. Something more exotic, raw, and...broken.

I realize that now. I was attracted to the broken side of her before I even knew what the fuck that was.

When Alexander said we were to be engaged, I thought I'd hit the jackpot.

If it hadn't been for her cold, aloof reaction.

I lean my head over and suck her bottom lip into my mouth like I did at twelve when she was sleeping in our guest house.

A shudder goes through her as I brush my lips against hers one last time. "You'll never escape me, my ugly monster."

TEN

Reina

My mouth is dry.

That's the first thought I have as I open my eyes. All thoughts of being thirsty disappear when I make out my surroundings.

I'm lying in a queen-sized bed with sheets that aren't my own. The white light in the ceiling isn't from my room either.

I jerk to a sitting position and check under the covers. I'm still wearing my clothes from earlier. Thank God.

Slowly, I inch to the edge, and my toes get swallowed by the plush carpet.

Where is this place? Wasn't I at the cottage not two seconds ago?

The time on the nightstand reads eight in the evening. I frown. It's been hours. How the hell has it been hours? I was standing there, taking a trip into the past and trying to remember my life and…

I gasp, covering my mouth with my hands.

All the memories that hit me earlier consume me once more. Mom's death. Reina's sacrifice. The fact that I confiscated another person's name.

This must be why I didn't feel comfortable with the name Reina Ellis when I woke up in the hospital with wiped memories.

I lived as Rai Sokolov for twelve years. That name resonated with me better, but I had to erase it. I had to become Reina to survive.

Just like that, I took her life and threw her into mine.

Those Russians were after Mom and me. Or rather, they were after me since they had no problem hurting Mom once they found me.

Tears fill my eyes as I fall back on the bed, my limbs shaking and my heart racing louder and harder with every second.

Mom.

Reina.

Dad.

They're all gone now, and I'm the only one who remains, the dirty little monster Rai who took an identity and a life that was never hers, who got engaged to a person who was never supposed to be hers.

Rai Sokolov.

That's Russian, like Mom's name and those men's accents.

Mom used to teach me some Russian, telling me it was better to understand my enemies so I'd know what I was in for.

She considered them enemies and ran away from them.

She took Reina and me and planned to leave the country. We had forged passports and forged identities and papers. But that day, they found us and everything blew up.

They killed Mom and took Reina.

I hate myself for being a fucking coward back then, for letting Reina take my place, for running away to Dad. I hate that I never looked back, never stopped.

In my twelve-year-old mind, I was so tired of running all the time, tired of never staying in one place for more than a few months, never having friends, never having enough food.

Never having a father.

I was also so fucking scared when I realized Mom no longer existed. She had been the one who took care of me, and I had no clue what the fuck to do without her.

So when Reina gave me her life, I took it.

I didn't ask her to run with me to Dad, because I knew they'd never stop until they got Mia Sokolov's daughter.

And they did stop. Once I started living with Dad, they never bothered me—I think. My memories are still fuzzy around that.

What I know for sure is that at the time, I thought Dad would try to find Reina and bring her back.

He must've realized he got the wrong twin. And in some way, maybe Dad searched for her. It can't be a coincidence that he was involved in all that dangerous business with the mafia.

Then they took him, too.

And they came back for Reina and me when we reunited at the cottage. Although I don't remember exactly what happened, I'm sure they did.

If they didn't kill her after all these years, surely they need her alive, right? Surely she's still out there.

Human remains.

A tear slides down my cheek and I quickly wipe it away.

No.

I won't believe they took her life. They need her in some way. She managed to survive all this time and will continue to do so.

You promised, Reina.

The door clicks open and I startle, nearly toppling over the side of the bed. During my jumbled thoughts about what happened, I forgot about the unfamiliar place I'm in.

My heart picks up speed and sweat beads on my forehead. My muscles tighten like every time Mom ushered me from the bed and told me we were leaving.

No warning, no nothing.

My eyes were usually closed as we ran in the middle of the night to God knows where then slept under the walls when we had no money for hotels. At least I slept—Mom never did. She'd stay wide awake all night watching over me to ward off any homeless.

Or the men chasing us.

Those motherfuckers, she called them. *They'll never take you away from me, Rai. Not as long as I breathe.*

What if they came for me now? What if they figured out the identity switch and decided to rectify their mistake nine years later?

A shadow spills into the room and I jump back, my shoulder blades hitting the wall.

The light casts a halo on him as he becomes clear. A long breath heaves out of my lips before they turn shallow again.

Asher.

No idea why it's both relieving and suffocating to see him.

Probably because he tried to kill you, Reina.

No, not Reina. Rai. I was always Rai. Reina was temporary. Her life was never mine to confiscate.

Maybe that's why I've been that cold and aloof with her personality. I didn't want people to get close because I didn't want to form any attachments. I was an imposter and knew that one day, the real Reina would return to her life.

I was only a watchdog, and in my attempts to remain detached, I royally fucked it up.

Asher carries a plate in his hands as he approaches me at a steady pace. His dark jeans hang low on his hips and his T-shirt tightens around the developed muscles of his chest.

I force myself to look away as a potent feeling of disgust grips me by the throat.

The reality of what I've done—and can't undo—slams against my face.

I fucked my sister's fiancé.

I lusted after him and clung to him as if I had every right to. Not only that, I also did something so unforgivable, he's thinking about killing me now.

What the fuck have I done?

He sits on the edge of the bed, setting the tray beside him. "You haven't eaten since this morning."

My stomach clenches as if approving of the statement. It's then I realize I'm still flattened against the wall, facing away as if my life depends on it.

"Where am I?" I ask without meeting his gaze.

"At your apartment." His voice is neutral, emotionless even. "Now sit down and eat."

I head to the entrance. Once I find my purse and phone, I'm leaving. Why the hell did he bring me to the apartment anyway? I barely get away with avoiding him in the large house where everyone else is.

"Stop and turn around." He speaks so low, goosebumps erupt on my skin. "You don't want me to do it for you."

You know what? Why should I keep on running away? I did enough of that for a lifetime when I was a kid.

The world needs to stop and face me this time. People need to see me, not Rai or Reina, a Sokolov or an Ellis, but me.

Just *me*.

The person inside who's barely holding on by a thread.

With a resigned sigh, I turn around and march over to where Asher sits on the bed.

My bed.

There's something so intimate about that, and I don't want to admit it right now.

I lower myself opposite him, with the plate between us. I place both my hands underneath my thighs so they don't act out on any crazy ideas like reaching out to brush back that stray strand on his forehead.

"Now eat," he orders.

God, this man and his authoritative streak. I wish I hated it.

If I did, maybe all of this would be easier. Maybe my entire body wouldn't be on high alert with a full rush of adrenaline.

"I'm fine." My stomach growls as soon as the words come out of my mouth.

Damn traitor.

"You were saying?" He raises an eyebrow.

"I don't want to eat, okay?" I pause. "Why did you bring me here? How did you find me anyway?"

"I followed you."

I followed you.

Just like that. No explanation, no attempt at apologizing.

Who am I kidding? I'm starting to think Asher isn't apologetic about anything.

He's his own brand of atypical, not exactly a sociopath, but something similar. At times, it feels like he does care, but at other times, he completely eradicates that part.

"And why are we here?" I murmur.

"Because." He takes a spoonful of what seems to be mac and cheese and places it in front of my mouth. "For the last time, fucking eat."

I glare at him, tempted to throw the entire plate at his face, but that's no excuse to waste good food.

Besides, I *am* hungry.

I try to take the spoon from him, but he keeps it away.

"Open your mouth."

"I'm not a kid, Ash. I can eat on my own."

"You lost your choice when you were acting like a brat." He shakes his head with a sigh. "And it's Asher, for fuck's sake."

My eyes cast downward. He's right; I don't have the right to call him that, to give him any nicknames or to let him feed me.

He's not mine.

He's Reina's.

That's why Old Reina always kept him at arm's length and pushed him away. I can understand her thought process more clearly now.

"Are you going to open your mouth, or should I do it for you?" His eyes darken with malice, and I gulp at the punishing promise in them.

He'll definitely make me, and I have no doubt that I won't like my reaction to it.

I slowly part my lips. The spoon clinks against my teeth as he gently shoves it inside. My pulse rises in my throat and I barely chew before swallowing the mac and cheese. It tastes rich and strong, but I barely focus on that.

Oh, God. This is so intimate. I shouldn't be doing it with Asher.

I reach out for the spoon, but he keeps it out of reach and forces me to eat from his hand.

There's something changed about his expression, something curious and new.

Or maybe my brain is interpreting it that way after all I uncovered about the past and my identity.

Asher's eyes keep darkening every time I wrap my lips around the spoon to swallow the pasta. His jaw ticks and he feeds me slower, as if savoring the moment.

The air thickens with tension, the scene taking an entirely different direction. It's like he's fucking my mouth instead of feeding me. At first, it's with his thumb, and then it'll be with his cock.

My cheeks flame at the thought. That's not right to imagine—at all.

And yet, my thighs clench together. The leather of

my skirt becomes too harsh against my heated skin and my T-shirt turns tight over my hardening nipples.

No.

I need to pull myself out of this trance.

"Are you going to tell me why we're here?" I ask after swallowing another spoonful of the food.

"Mac and cheese was your favorite when you were younger," he says, as if it's the perfect answer to my question.

"Don't many kids love it?"

"Not you." He raises an eyebrow. "You used to feel peevy around it until I once dared you to eat it, and then you secretly fell in love."

For a second, I think my heart will abandon me and stop beating. Is he talking about Reina versus me? "When was that? How old was I?"

"Right before your thirteenth birthday." The spoon clinks against the bowl as he fills it. "Why are you asking?"

"Nothing."

So it was me, not Reina. A strange sense of relief floods me. It's so sudden and strong, I briefly close my eyes until it goes away.

My unfamiliarity with mac and cheese makes sense. Mom was Russian and never made it. I wasn't exposed to the typical American life until I lived with Dad.

"What were you doing in that cottage, Reina?" His tone hardens like that time in the hospital when he asked me if I was running away from him.

"Searching for the truth," I say, my eyes cast downward.

I can't look at him, not when he thinks I'm Reina.

You're an imposter.

You should die.

The gloomy cloud roams around my head like a halo, trying to swallow me inside and suck out my soul.

"What truth?" He pushes another spoonful in my mouth. "And when I talk to you, look at me."

I shake my head, stomach in knots as I swallow. "I'm full. Can I go back now?"

"Answer the question and look at me," he deadpans.

I remain rooted in place, mute.

"Don't fucking test me or I swear—"

"Or what?" My head snaps up, fully meeting that forest gaze that has more depth than any human should be allowed to. "You'll attempt to kill me like on the roof, in the classroom, or in the locker room? I know it was you. I heard what you said to Arianna on her death anniversary. I know you'll make me pay for whatever the fuck I did. So stop pretending you care for me, whether I eat or starve, whether I lock myself in my room and die, or whether I disappear into the forest and never return. Just stop fucking pretending!"

Because it's fucking with my head more than everything else he's done, and I'm not in a position to have my head fucked with.

I expected Asher to be surprised after my sudden outburst, but he reveals nothing. His expression remains completely blank as he drops the spoon into the bowl on the tray between us.

Then he laughs. It's long and humorless and shoots something akin to raw fear down my spine.

This is Asher uncut.

This is Asher without an ounce of holding back.

"Pretending." His laughter finally subsides, replaced by a closed-off expression. "Fucking pretending."

"Well, wasn't it?" I fold my arms over my chest, my nails digging into the skin. "You only pretended just to get closer to me and screw me over. You made me believe you were my savior when you were the villain all along."

"Drop your arms," he growls.

"What?"

"Don't give me that high-and-mighty Reina act. I'm not everyone else, so don't you dare put up your walls with me, and drop your fucking arms when you're talking to me."

"No." I jut out my chin.

I need my arms around my chest. I need protection and walls. I need everything I can get when I'm dealing with Asher.

"No?" he repeats.

"No."

He pushes the tray to the side and grabs my forearm, shoving it down in front of me. His nose nearly touches mine as he speaks, his tone low and threatening. "You can make this easy or hard, my ugly monster."

"What does it matter when you're going to kill me?" I wish my voice were full of contempt and anger or the stabbing betrayal. Instead, it's almost like resignation to a cruel fate.

This is karma biting me in the ass for stealing Reina's life and throwing her under the bus.

I had to fall for her psycho fiancé just so he'd plan to kill me.

Wait...no. I didn't fall for Asher. I can totally get over him.

Right?

"Since when did you become such a coward?" He's still

in my face, so when he speaks, I smell sandalwood and citrus, and I feel his pulse about to join my erratic one.

His words hit me harder than they should. My ears heat and everything in me revolts against it.

I'm not a coward; I'm a fighter.

I fought all this time, didn't I? With Mom and with Reina and then with Dad and without him. I'm still fighting. I'm still trying to chase the gloomy cloud away.

Cowards don't do that.

Ever.

"Screw you." I push him away and jump from the bed then storm to the balcony's door.

The moment I slide it open, a gust of strong wind slaps me in the face. Wind is good. Wind is as angry as I feel and as lost, too, never sure where to settle or how to go about it.

There are two chairs and a table at the far end of the balcony. I hop on the chair and then onto the table near the edge just as Asher stalks out after me.

I'm facing him, one leg planted on the railing's edge and the other on the table. We're at least thirty stories high. If I fall, I'll die.

Everything will fucking end.

I shake the gloomy thoughts away and face Asher.

He freezes in the doorway, shoving both hands in his pockets, and I can almost swear he fists them. "What the fuck are you doing, Reina?"

"That's the thing, Ash. I was never Reina."

"*What?*"

"My name is Rai Sokolov and I'm Reina's twin sister. I switched places with her when we were twelve. After Mom kidnapped her, we took each other's identity. She went with the Russian mafia that chased me and I came to live with Dad." I don't know why I'm telling him all this, but now that I've started, I can't stop. "I'm not from your world. I'm just a runaway, a nobody who couldn't save her own sister. So if you want to kill me for whatever the fuck I did to you, stop playing games and do it already. Or let me do it for you—I don't care anymore."

The whole time I've been talking, Asher has been slowly approaching me, gradually removing both hands from his pockets.

I should've focused on that and on the fact that he's probably coming to make what I asked reality.

My limbs shake and my leg keeps approaching the edge. The strong wind hits me in the bones, my teeth chatter, and a full-body tremor takes me over.

"Come down from there, Reina." Asher's order is slow but firm enough to make my heart jump.

"Didn't you hear a word I said? I told you I'm not Reina. I'm an imposter."

"I don't give a fuck about your name. You're the only Reina I know." He reaches out his hand. "Come the fuck down."

I eye him suspiciously. "Don't you want me dead?"

"Come down. *Now*." His face becomes closed off like he's an entirely different person, almost as if he's camouflaging something.

Then I recognize that somber look in his eyes.

Fear.

Pure, raw fear.

He doesn't want me to jump.

Why the hell is my heart thumping at that?

Stop it. Don't celebrate. Don't you dare celebrate.

"If…" I clear my throat. "If you don't want me dead just yet, can you let me search for my sister first? I'll do whatever you want once I find her."

He says nothing.

"Please…" I soften my voice.

He grabs me by the wrist and pulls me down so hard I shriek, thinking I'll topple over the edge.

Instead, I land in the midst of strong arms. Steel limbs crush me to his chest, his embrace nearly suffocating and yet so…warm.

Asher is warm when he chooses to be. It's just that he rarely allows that part to shine through.

My cheek lies against his chest muscles and I inhale him, the sandalwood and citrus, the warmth and the safety.

The need to cry hits me out of nowhere.

But why?

Why, Asher, just why?

He places both hands on my cheeks and wrenches me away from his warmth to hold me at arm's length. "Don't you dare fucking do that again, understood?"

My lips tremble, but I say nothing.

"What happened to what you said? The part about how I don't deserve for you to sacrifice yourself for me or anyone else?" He shakes me hard as if he's jamming those words inside me. "Snap the fuck out of it."

The need to throw myself into his embrace again becomes overwhelming like an actual presence with thoughts and feelings, but since I can't do that, I focus on my other purpose. "Are you going to let me search for my sister?"

"For fuck's sake." He wrenches himself away from me

and I flinch backward as he turns, facing the endless buildings and their lights.

His shoulders hunch with tension, and I don't know how to make it better—not that I should.

"So?" I press instead.

"Fine."

A breath heaves out of me as I try to get my chaotic feelings in check. If he leaves me be, I'll be able to focus on finding Reina.

Then, when I give her back her life, I'll pay whatever price Asher wants of me.

"But you're not doing it alone," he continues.

"What?"

He turns around, his expression less agitated than earlier. All tension has left him, replaced by a calculative streak.

"We're in this together."

My brows furrow. "Why would you want to help me?"

He reaches me in two seconds and wraps a hand around my neck. "Because I own you, my ugly monster."

ELEVEN

Reina

We stay the night in my apartment after Asher refused my millionth attempt to make him leave.
He even called Izzy, informing her I'd be spending the night with friends.

Friends. Psh, whatever.

Asher is probably the last person who could be considered my friend.

I spy on him as he washes the dishes in the kitchen—without using the dishwasher. Then he places the leftover mac and
cheese in a casserole and puts that in the refrigerator.

Seriously, why does he keep doing things like that for me?
It only makes me feel more apprehensive.

I retreat to where I woke up and close the door. It's so similar to my room in Alex's house, only this one's closet is filled with
leather skirts and pants, the latest fashionable bags and shoes.

With a sigh, I lie on the bed and stare at the ceiling. My

phone and bag sit on the nightstand. Asher must've brought them in when he carried me up here.

I unlock Instagram then type.

Reina-Ellis: Are you there?

His reply is immediate.

Cloud003: For you, always.

A smile tugs on my lips. I need a friend so bad right now, and I don't want to bother Naomi or Lucy with a long story this late.

Sure, I could've called Jace, but this anonymity gives me a lot of courage.

Reina-Ellis: I stood on the edge of a roof today and threatened to kill myself. I didn't mean to, you know. I only wanted to bargain for something else, but as I stood there, a pull kept tugging me.

Cloud003: Did you give in to it?

This is what I like about him. He doesn't judge me when I talk about this type of stuff.

Reina-Ellis: No, or I wouldn't be talking to you right now *tongue out emoji*

My attempt at humor falls flat.

Cloud003: But you thought about it.

Reina-Ellis: I did, but at the same time, I didn't.

Cloud003: How so?

Reina-Ellis: I can't explain it. There was someone else with me, and as I stood there, I felt a strange type of

freedom and told him things I've been keeping a secret for nine years, things no one else knows, things I don't think I would've ever said if I weren't standing at the edge. There's something so liberating about having nothing left to lose.

He takes a few seconds to reply.

Cloud003: And what was his reaction?

I bite my lower lip. I don't want to tell him about Asher or about my double identity, but at the same time, I want to continue talking to him.

He brings me calm.

Reina-Ellis: He didn't like it.

Cloud003: He didn't like what?

Reina-Ellis: Me standing on the ledge and threatening to jump.

It hits me then.

Arianna's death. Oh my God—Arianna died the same way, and I just repeated the scene in front of him.

In my mind, I thought he wouldn't care, but that look he gave me was the complete opposite of not caring.

He was on the verge of himself.

Reina-Ellis: Shit. I think I hurt him. What do I do?

Cloud003: Why are you asking me?

Cloud003: I don't appreciate you talking about other men, my slut.

I roll my eyes.

The door bangs open.

I jerk, hugging the phone to my chest as if Asher could see my conversation with Jason. I mean, it's not cheating. We're friends.

So why the hell am I hiding the phone?

No, I'm not hiding it. I just don't want Asher to see what I said about him.

He closes the door, trapping us both in the room as he leans against it. The soft lamplight casts a shadow on his darkened features, almost making them frightening.

Scratch that. They *are* frightening.

Although I feel lighter now that he knows I'm not Reina, Asher is still one of the villains in my story—if not the most dangerous.

I don't feel drawn to other villains. I don't clench my thighs upon seeing them like some high school girl with a crush.

"What…" My voice comes out breathy, and I clear my throat. "What are you doing here?"

He doesn't answer and stalks toward me instead. His steps are slow, measured, and filled with so much sexual energy it radiates in the air and wraps a noose around my neck.

I hug the phone tighter to my chest, as if it can save me from Asher's hold and teleport me out of here.

"What were you doing?" His question drifts like smoke without fire, impenetrable and asphyxiating.

"Nothing." My voice is defensive and too loud, even to my own ears.

"Is that so?" He's suddenly standing beside me, and I have to gaze up to look at him.

His heat radiates on my skin in waves and I can't look away. I can't do anything except stare like an idiot.

As I'm caught in his trance, he reaches over and snatches

my phone away. His brows scrunch as he studies the screen, but there's no other indication of his mood.

I finally shake myself out of my stupor and yank my phone back.

It's too late, though. He must've seen the name, or worse, the last few lines of my conversation with Jason.

My ears and face flame with shame. Is it supposed to feel this crippling?

"Are you cheating on me, Reina?" His question is like a slap across my face. My cheek is hot and tingling where his imaginary hand struck me.

"N-No." My lips tremble around the word.

Although I might have cheated before, I don't now and will never do it again.

Why the hell did I cheat? Was it another way to remain detached and not grow close to Asher? Because I know—I'm sure—I felt something for him in the past.

These intense feelings didn't spring up out of nowhere. They've been magnifying over the years, and when I finally had the freedom of amnesia, I just let them loose.

I let them consume me alive.

He leans over so his entire body is angled toward mine. "Why do I think you did?"

"What about you, then?" I cover my ignorance by jutting out my chin. "Didn't you cheat on me?"

"No."

"Do you expect me to believe that?"

"I don't care what you believe. I don't have the time or energy to focus on anyone else."

My heartbeat hammers faster as his words sink in. He just admitted that he only has the time and energy to focus on me.

Even if it's the most fucked-up type of focus.

"Not even in England?" I murmur.

"Not even in England."

Well, shit. How does he have the power to make my pulse race this hard and fast? Is it a curse?

Or maybe it's something stronger I refuse to admit.

"So, are you?" he repeats. "Cheating on me, I mean."

"No." I say the word with an odd type of conviction like I never cheated on him, like the thought never even crossed my mind.

"Good, because I don't react well to others touching what I own." His finger glides along my cheek, leaving goosebumps in its wake as he traces my lower lip in a sensual caress. "You're mine, aren't you, prom queen?"

Prom queen.

My chest flutters in and out of sync.

I don't know why I love it so much when he calls me that. Could be because it's neither Reina nor Rai. It's neither identity theft nor confusion.

It's just me.

His thumb and forefinger squeeze my chin. "Answer me."

"I don't belong to someone who wants to hurt me."

I might be inexplicably attracted to Asher, but I've never, not once, forgotten what he did to me. That fear was wild and raw and I can almost feel how I hung on the roof or how these same fingers choked me with the intent of ending my life.

People think when you have dark thoughts about ending your own life, you'd feel relieved when someone else takes the burden away and finishes it for you.

It's not true, at least not for me.

That terror I felt back then still pulses beneath my skin,

pumping in my bloodstream. Those were some of the rare moments where I thought I didn't want to die, that I couldn't leave just like that.

I don't think I'll ever forget that type of horror.

"Oh, but you do." Asher's hand travels down until it wraps around my throat. "You fucking do."

"But—"

He squeezes, cutting off my air supply and my words. "Shut up, don't talk about that. Not tonight."

Not tonight? What the hell is that supposed to mean?

Still gripping my neck, his thumb strokes up and down my pulse point as if soothing it, feeling it, making sure it's there.

There's something about the way he holds my throat prisoner. Sometimes, it's harsh, dominant, and meant to prove a point. Other times, like right now, it's almost…tender, meant to establish a connection.

"You'll never do shit like that on the balcony again, understood?" He's not boring his eyes into mine. Instead, his entire attention is on my neck.

What is his problem exactly? He's acting strangely for someone who's been actively trying to end my life.

When I don't answer—partially because he's barely allowing me air to breathe, let alone talk—he wraps his other hand at the back of my head and forces me to nod, up and down.

"That's a yes. That's, I'll never do it again, Asher. I won't allow people to see me that way."

He releases me then, both his hands pulling away from me. A funny type of emptiness prickles on my skin as if I don't want him gone.

Why the hell do I not want him gone?

He stalks to the foot of the bed and I watch his every move. The word 'stay' is at the tip of my tongue, but I don't say it.

Snap out of it, Reina or Rai or whoever the fuck you are.

I expect him to leave, but he turns around. The dangerous lust on his face takes me by surprise as he reaches for me.

"What—"

Words die at the back of my throat when he grabs both my ankles in his strong, merciless hold and pulls me toward him in one ruthless tug.

The phone falls from my hand, clattering to the ground. My legs fly open and the leather skirt bunches up my thighs, barely covering my butt.

Asher kneels on the ground as both my legs hang helplessly on his broad shoulders.

"What are you doing?" I gasp, my voice breathy and choppy like I've been running.

"You had your dinner. It's time I have mine."

I hardly process his words as he tugs my skirt up around my waist and yanks my panties down. A gust of air covers my core and my spine jerks.

A groan tears out of him as he widens my legs to watch me closer. "You're wet. Why the fuck are you soaked, prom queen?"

I don't know. I really don't know. It's baffling even to my own brain. Something about me is wired wrong, and I have no idea what it is.

Or maybe I do know, but I don't want to admit it even to myself.

He runs his middle finger along my slit, ripping a whimper from me. "You were hardly wet before, if ever. You never moaned, either, or shook with desire like you do now."

The confession doesn't lessen my reaction. If anything, it

makes my limbs shake harder like a leaf in the wind outside the windows.

He slides his middle finger up and down again before he thrusts it inside me and murmurs against my slick folds. "You changed."

In the beginning, I also thought I'd changed, but now I realize that's not the case.

Losing my memories allowed me to let myself loose, to not think about confiscating Reina's life, and for that reason, it seems as if I've changed when the truth is, I was just releasing my bottled-up feelings.

"I like the new you." His voice rumbles as he glides his tongue from the bottom of my clit up.

Oh, God.

His confession along with his touch grips my body like a possession, nearly pushing me off the edge.

"Just so we're clear." He nibbles on my sensitive skin with his teeth, sending rolling pleasure to my belly. "This. Pussy. Belongs. To. Me."

With every word, he bites, making me writhe and squirm on the bed.

"You belong to me, prom queen. Now say it." He thrusts his tongue into my entrance and my thighs quiver with the building pleasure coiling at the bottom of my stomach.

He thrusts in and out of me as if he's filling me with his cock, as if he's punishing me, teaching me my place, and eating me alive.

In the midst of all that, he's bringing me shattering pleasure, the type that turns me mindless and blind. There's too much intensity, too much control.

Just too much.

He teases my swollen clit with his thumb, continuing his ruthless assault.

Sparks fill my vision as my head rolls back and my nails dig into the sheets on either side of me.

"Oh…oh…"

"That's not the word." He slaps the inner flesh of my thigh in such an erotic way that it makes me gasp for air. "Now, say it."

I gulp, trying to gather enough energy to speak.

He slaps my ass this time, and my mouth opens in a wordless cry. Shit. Why the hell is that such a turn-on?

"Last." *Slap.* "Chance."

My body jerks off the bed as I choke out the words. "I…I belong to you. Only you."

"Repeat that." He slaps me again, the hardest he ever has, the sound echoing in the thick air.

I scream the words as stars form behind my lids. His tongue and fingers don't stop, bringing me a pleasure so wild it drains me of all thoughts and what-ifs.

All I can do is feel—his slight stubble, his wicked mouth, and his uncut intensity.

Just *him.*

My villain and my savior.

My damnation and my salvation.

The only person I ever told my secret.

His head lifts from between my thighs so his eyes lock with mine. They're filled with raw lust and mischievous sadism. "Only me."

I nod, barely catching my breath. The skin he slapped earlier is flaming and pulsing with the need to have his hand on my ass.

How can I want this man so much? This is so fucked up.

He disappears between my legs again, his breath tickling my hypersensitive skin.

"Ash...? What are you doing?"

"I just started my dinner." I can feel his smirk without seeing it. "I'm going to tongue-fuck you until you can no longer move, prom queen."

And then he makes good on his promise.

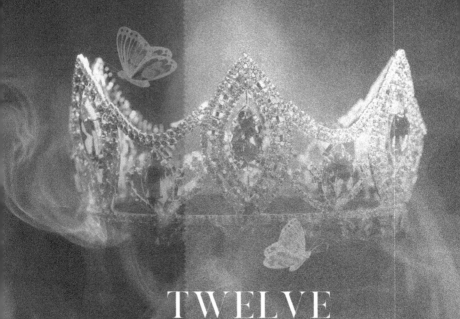

TWELVE

Reina

Asher takes me home in the morning.

We've barely talked since we woke up. Could be because of what happened last night—or everything that happened in the past.

After he wrenched three orgasms out of me with his tongue and fingers, I kind of passed out. The stimuli messed with my sensitive core, and I begged him to stop, sobbing through one orgasm after another.

Asher being Asher, he didn't.

My voice turned hoarse and I thought I was getting de-hydrated by the time he emerged from between my trembling legs and let them fall to the bed.

I was too spent to open my eyes, so I fell asleep right away.

When I opened my eyes in the morning, I was covered and comfy, but there was no sign that he'd slept beside me. He must've gone back to the living room or the guest room.

My heart still has that slight ache at the thought—not that I want him to sleep with me. That's beside the whole point of avoiding him.

Currently, he drives with ease, one hand on the wheel and the other on his thigh. No words. No nothing.

I chat with Naomi and Lucy in our group chat the entire way. It's a useless attempt to distract myself from Asher; my mind keeps dragging me back to him anyway.

His presence is impossible to ignore or deny. He's like a constant, unmovable and unchangeable.

I peek at him through my lashes, at his styled hair and thick brows, at his chiseled jaw and firm lips that kissed me in intimate places and brought me to the highest throes of pleasure.

My cheeks heat and I shake myself internally to chase away the image. What's wrong with me? This isn't the time to think about that.

Besides, he hasn't mentioned it once this morning. Maybe he regrets it.

Why does that fill me with so much trepidation?

I mean, I should regret it, too, but I can't find it in me to do that.

We make it to the house's driveway. It's still early in the morning so a few staff are mingling around the garden.

I reach out a hand to release my seatbelt. Asher grabs it in his, startling me.

"W-what is it?" I halt midway, my pulse skyrocketing.

"We'll talk to Alexander," he says.

I nod. That's what I've been planning to do. He obviously knows about the business Dad did with the mafia, and he must know something about my sister.

"After he tells you what you want to know, you'll tell him you're moving back to your apartment."

"Why?" My voice sounds as spooked as I feel.

"I don't care to share you." His grip tightens around my wrist. "You belong to me, remember?"

My heart suddenly resurrects back to life, beating and thumping so wildly it's impossible to keep up. It's as if it's been dead since the morning and Asher just gave it a reason to be alive.

He really needs to stop saying things like that if all he ever plans to do is hurt me. He needs to stop touching me, calling me his, and looking at me with those intense eyes that seem ready to strip me bare and devour me all over again. My brain is starting to disregard the danger and focus on those small gestures, on what his body is saying instead of what his mind is planning.

"What if I don't want to move out?" I ask. "People are after me."

It's a lie. I want to get out of this place filled with others. I think I'll be more comfortable when I'm alone. After all, that's the reason Old Reina moved out as soon as she was legal.

I'm starting to connect to Reina in more ways than one, and I have no idea how that makes me feel.

"If they were actively after you, they could've easily removed you from campus." He sounds thoughtful. "Ask Alexander to tighten up security at the apartment building."

"You don't get to tell me what to do, Ash." I pull my wrist from his hold and fold my arms.

The glare he shoots my way is so harsh I squirm in my seat. "What did I say about that?"

"Fine." I unfold my arms. "But you still don't get to tell me what to do."

"Is that a dare?" His voice lowers. "By the end of the night, you'll beg me to tell you what to do."

I don't miss the meaning behind his words, and my face must turn a deep shade of red.

"Look at you blushing." His finger traces along my cheek in a sensual caress, his expression filled with awe.

I love it when I catch him off guard like that. A powerful sensation rushes through me at the thought that I have this effect on him.

Still, he's an arrogant bastard right now.

Swatting his hand away, I adapt my no-nonsense tone. "I have friends here, you know, like Izzy and Jason. We have Scrabble nights."

"Fuck Scrabble nights." His face hardens as he leans closer. "Keep the fuck away from Jason."

"Uh…no. He's my friend."

His hand shoots between my thighs, cupping me through my jeans. I gasp, my eyes nearly bulging out of their sockets. Tingles erupt where he touches me and my body's memory kicks into gear. All I can think about is his face, fingers, and tongue down there.

"This is mine." His lips are mere inches away from my face, a slight deviation and they'd meet mine. He speaks in a gravelly voice that shoots a shudder up my spine. "You're *mine*, and I don't appreciate people threatening what belongs to me. If you let anyone take liberties with you, I won't stay still. Am I making myself clear, prom queen?"

I couldn't speak even if I tried to. His closeness and the scent of his aftershave mixed with sandalwood and citrus is doing crazy things to my senses, heightening them, crushing them against one another.

It's chaos.

Beautiful, maddening chaos.

Just like Asher.

"I said." His grip turns merciless, and so freaking dominant. "Am I making myself clear?"

I nod once, not because I completely agree, but because I don't want to test him while he's in such a state. It's like he's gasoline waiting for a spark so he can erupt and burn everything in his vicinity.

While I do want to witness different parts of Asher, I don't want to get on his bad side right now. He's the only one who knows about Reina, and I might need his help to find my sister.

"Good." He releases me and opens the door. "You have two days to move back to your apartment."

I groan as the door closes behind him.

Arrogant bastard.

Alex keeps checking his watch as Asher and I sit in his office.

From what I've learned about him so far, his firm is his God and he has no other religion than work. Maybe that's why he and Asher don't see eye to eye on anything.

My supposed fiancé touches my leg with his. Great, so I'll be the only one doing the talking.

Asher's nudge is basically telling me I need to start soon because Alex is getting restless.

He sits behind his huge mahogany desk that's crowded with endless paperwork. I don't even know what his use is for all that at home.

"Reina," he starts. "You mentioned wanting to talk to me? We can do this after I return."

"I remember a few things," I say, calmly but loud enough for him to hear me.

Alex grabs a retractable pen from the desk and stops checking his watch. "Go on."

"I remember a twin sister and a mother and how we ran away in my childhood. As for that night, I think I was attacked after I reunited with my sister."

Silence.

Alex continues watching me as if he's deciding whether or not he can erase those memories from my brain all over again.

"Did you tell her anything?" Alex's question is directed to his son. His voice hardens when he speaks to Asher, like he's talking to a mortal enemy, not his flesh and blood.

"I know nothing to tell," Asher says casually.

My gaze bounces between father and son as I try to make sense of their words. Asher knows something?

I tighten my hands in my lap, my nails digging into the skin of my palms. "Can anyone tell me what's going on?"

"I suppose you should know." Alex sighs. "Ignorance never did you any good before."

No, it wasn't ignorance. Even if Dad and Alex hid the truth from me, I think I knew it deep down. That's why I searched for Reina and found her on my own. I meant to escape with her.

That's not something an ignorant person would do.

"Your mother was the bratva's Pakhan's daughter. Mia Sokolov, daughter of Nikolai Sokolov and cousin of Ivan Sokolov."

Those names are familiar.

Oh my God.

They can't possibly be…

"They're big names in the states and in Russia." Alex clicks his pen. "Gareth didn't know about Mia's origins when he got together with her more than two decades ago. She ran away from home and he just took her in. Of course, her father and cousin didn't stop searching for her. She sullied the family's name by running away. When they found out about her relationship with Gareth, they ordered their henchmen to kill your father."

My lips part but no sound comes out.

"Mia and Gareth agreed to break it off for both their sakes. By that time, Mia was already pregnant with you and your sister. Your parents agreed that each would get a twin before they parted ways. Of course, Nikolai and Ivan weren't having it. They only agreed to let Gareth keep one of the twins if he allowed the bratva a share in his business, and he agreed."

A tremor shoots through my limbs at the thought of what my parents went through.

"And the other twin?" I gulp. "What happened to her?"

"Mia took her and ran, but Nikolai wanted the girl as his heir. Considering that Mia was the only offspring he had, her daughter needed to be brought up as the bratva's princess."

"And Mom didn't want that." It's not a question; it's a statement.

That's why we were on the run for twelve years. The forged identities and the late-night escapes make sense now.

Mom didn't want me to be the Russian mafia's princess. She must've lived that role her entire life and couldn't accept having her daughter go through that fate.

Her diligence and quick wit make sense, too. She knew their ways well enough to be able to escape them for twelve whole years.

"She didn't, and Nikolai wasn't happy." Alex sighs. "After she disappeared without a trace, he began to pester Gareth about taking the other twin, which, of course, he refused. However, Nikolai's intentions must've reached Mia because she kidnapped her other daughter from school. She planned to take you both out of the country and away from her father's organization."

"But they found us first." My eyes well with tears and a hand presses on my thigh.

Asher.

I'd forgotten he was here. My lips pull in a small smile as I take in his silent support.

I didn't know I needed him beside me until now.

Alex clears his throat, and I focus back on him. "Yes. I assume it was easier for her to run with one, but the two of you slowed her down."

"Why would..." I suck in a breath. "Why would my grandfather order his only daughter killed?"

"That's the problem—he didn't. Nikolai would've never hurt Mia no matter how much he threatened to. She must've resisted, and her death was an accident—or at least that's what I thought."

I shift to the edge of the couch. "What do you mean?"

"After the Russians took your sister and you returned to live with Gareth, he didn't stop looking into ways to save her. He even had a few spies on the inside. From what we learned, Ivan, Nikolai's nephew and Mia's cousin, didn't like the fact that the Pakhan was handing his business to a girl. Well, and her future husband, but that's beside the point. Since Mia ran away, he's been plotting to take Nikolai down, eradicate all his descendants, and take over."

"You...you think he killed Mom on purpose?"

"I'm almost sure he did. She was in his way and he needed her gone, so he disguised it as if she killed herself." His eyes soften. "I'm sorry."

I swallow back the tears, my chest splintering into pieces at the revelation. All Mom ever wanted was to save us from the monstrous life she lived, and she had to pay the price with her life.

"Then why didn't he kill her daughter, too?" I ask.

"I assume because one of Nikolai's most trusted men grabbed her first. As soon as she was with her grandfather, even Ivan wouldn't have been able to hurt her."

"So Reina is safe with Nikolai?" I whisper.

Alex pauses mid-press of his retractable pen. "I see, so you remember that, too."

"You knew?" Asher's snarl causes my limbs to shake more.

"Of course I do." Alex goes back to clicking his pen. "Gareth was my partner. We shared everything."

"So Dad knew, too." My murmur is pained, barely audible.

I figured he'd realize Reina and I switched places, but deep down, I hoped I'd be able to fly under the radar. My hand finds Asher's on my thigh and I grip it tight like it's a safety line. I don't dare look at him, silently hoping for his support. He threads his fingers through mine, and my lower lip trembles at the gesture.

"Yes," Alex says. "He was happy to get you back."

My head jerks up. "He...was?"

"Of course. He lived in guilt for letting you and your mother go all those years ago. He searched for you as diligently as Nikolai, but your mom was a professional at running."

I smile a little before it falls off. "But he lost Reina."

"Not really." Alex leans forward in his chair. "Nikolai let him see her now and again when they gathered for business.

Gareth also made sure she was living well, and she was. She loved Nikolai and he treated her well, like his princess."

Oh.

I didn't know that.

"Why didn't I get to meet her?" I ask.

"Nikolai's condition was that if you two got together again, it'd only be under the bratva's rules. Meaning, you could only reunite with her if Gareth gave you up, too. He wasn't ready for that."

I tighten my hands around each other. "Then something happened, right?"

"Well, yes." Alex clicks his pen. "Your father died in an accident, which I still think had Ivan's hands all over it. That little fucker always hated his guts."

"So Reina stayed on her own?"

"She had Nikolai and an insider Gareth put with her. He's a hitman of some secret organization who kills for the bratva. I've been in contact with him since Gareth's death." Alex pauses, as if trying to lessen the blow of what he's about to say next. "Nikolai got sick and died. I knew Ivan would try to kill Reina— Rai—as soon as he could to secure his position. I tried to have the insider get her out, but she wouldn't agree. I didn't know she was planning on meeting you or that you were still searching for her." Alex straightens, becoming tenfold bigger. "What happened that night, Reina?"

"We met…" I trail off. "I think I planned to escape with her."

Asher's hand tightens on my thigh and I wince as I keep my head down. He was right all along; I did plan to escape.

But it was bigger than Blackwood and any reason I had to hate him.

Or maybe it has everything to do with him after all.

"She said something about having business to finish and that she'd find me...I think."

How do I even remember that?

Alex gives a sharp nod. "She has Nikolai's ledger, which holds all the names, numbers, and dirt on the people he did business with. He announced before his death that the owner of that ledger is his sole heir. Ivan can't get the others' blessing to be Pakhan without that book. That's why he's hunting her down."

"So she's alive?" I nearly choke on my own breath.

"I believe so, yes." He rubs his chin. "I got a text from my guy that she was safe a day after your attack."

"Nothing after?"

"Unfortunately, no. But this guy wouldn't make any contact if he thought it would put Rai in danger. Besides, Ivan is flipping the city upside down to find her, so she must be on the run. I wouldn't be surprised if she got out of the country."

A breath leaves me, but it's not complete relief. Reina is still in danger. If this Ivan finds her, he'll take that ledger and skin her alive.

They torture people in the mafia.

They kill them in cold blood like they did to Mom.

"I'm hiring that security for you, Reina." Alex's tone becomes non-negotiable. "If Ivan thinks using you against Rai will bring her forward, he won't hesitate to beat you like the other time. Just because they're quiet doesn't mean they forgot."

"I agree," Asher says.

My spine shivers at the memory of pain all over my body.

This war is so much bigger than I thought.

THIRTEEN

Asher

It takes Reina three days to move out of Alexander's house.
Three fucking days.
She had to have a sappy goodbye with that fucker
Jason, who's starting to get on my nerves.

If I watch him put his arm around her one more time, I'm
breaking it and killing any chance of him going pro. Every time
he watches a game on TV, he'll think about me and wish he'd
never laid a hand on what's mine.

Reina had a small farewell gathering with Elizabeth and
the staff then made sure Alexander was good with her move
and that he stationed her new security at her apartment.

The old Reina would've never minded people surrounding her. She'd have made her decisions in a heartbeat and the
world could suffer.

Well, it turns out she's Rai or what-the-fuck-ever. I
should've known Alexander had all this information. I just never

thought he and Gareth could've hidden an identity switch this way.

Does her name matter? Does it change anything?

No, and fucking no.

I was never interested in Reina prior to her disappearance. The one I got entangled within all the wrong ways was the girl who returned with Gareth that day.

The girl who watched her surroundings every time she moved as if suspecting someone was chasing her. Turns out, she really had people chasing her all along.

I didn't know how to feel as I listened to her conversation with Alexander a few days ago. She suffered in her childhood and was a kid on the run with no one but her mother—and even that support was taken away.

It's sort of like Ari and me after Mom died.

No. I won't think about Ari.

That's the thought I've been pushing away since I found Reina unconscious in that cottage and after she nearly jumped off the balcony.

She almost fucking *jumped*.

My muscles tighten at the memory as if I can see her in front of me, shaking, eyes welling with tears and her leg threatening to give up on her.

Just like Ari.

I briefly close my eyes as I push the building's door open. The concierge nods in my direction. He knows better than to question me. After all, Alexander owns the whole damn thing.

True to his word, the man who calls himself my father got her security. They're stationed outside the building, and one of them is at the far end in the corner, near the concierge's desk.

Even the latter has some security training and would react fast in case of danger.

I press the button for the penthouse's floor and enter the code. As the doors close, I lean back, placing both hands in my pockets and letting my mind roam around the endless fucking possibilities that arose out of nowhere.

Reina will never be safe unless her sister is. Even if her sister is dead, there's no telling if Ivan will come after her. He'd want to eliminate the last descendent of Nikolai Sokolov's bloodline.

So far, only Reina remains.

And Rai.

She lived amongst them for years, so I'm hoping she has a trick or two up her sleeve like her mother did.

True, there's always that tiny possibility the twins switched back when they reunited that night. With the memory loss, Rai could've thought she was back to being Reina.

That possibility barely exists for me.

I recognize Reina no matter who or what she is. Her personality deviated a little—a lot—after the memory loss, but there are those few tells.

The way she shuts out the world by crossing her arms over her chest. The way she leads the cheerleading squad like she was born for it. How she dances, how she jumps, and how the corner of her mouth twitches when she smiles.

All those little details are enough evidence she's still the same. It's only that she's more spontaneous now, more *maddening*.

Sometimes, I have no fucking clue how to deal with her.

The door hisses open straight into her living room, and I push off the wall to step inside.

The lights are on, but there's no sign of her. I ignore the kitchen and go to her room. Reina would never cook even if you paid her for it. She says she doesn't know how to cook, but I'm starting to think maybe it's because she only knew Russian dishes before and didn't want to expose that detail about herself.

Soon, I'll get her to open up to me like she did on that balcony.

Like she always wanted to when we were pre-teens.

The sound of running water in the shower greets me as soon as I step into her room. Her clothes and purse lie on the chair in complete disorder.

I shake my head. Another thing about Reina? She can't get organized to save her life.

My cock twitches at the thought of joining her, making her jump in surprise, feasting on her blushing face, and then sinking into her warmth.

I can fuck her against the wall or on the floor.

That has to wait, though.

She defied me, and that won't go unnoticed. I sit on the edge of the bed, the same bed on which I had her for dinner—three times—before I exhausted the fuck out of her.

My cock strains against my jeans in remembrance. Since I started eating her pussy, I'm a fucking addict going through withdrawal.

The sound of the running water cuts off and soon after, she strolls inside. Reina doesn't notice me as she readjusts the tiny towel around her. It barely covers the swell of her tits and the curve of her ass.

Her wet hair falls on either side of her shoulders, dripping down her neck and the deep line between her tits.

My cock bulges in my pants as I watch her every movement. It takes all my self-restraint not to grab her, throw her on the ground, and fuck her like an animal.

The only reason I'm stopping is because she needs to pay first.

A small voice in the back of my head tells me I shouldn't be doing this. This isn't my plan. This isn't how Ari will rest in peace.

But I kill that voice like I always have since this new version of Reina woke up in the hospital, since she sucked my finger like she meant it, like she actually fucking *wanted* it.

A gasp falls from her lips as her gaze lands on mine. Those ocean-deep eyes, those eyes that could drown people with a look.

When I was a teenager, I yearned to own those eyes, to trap them somewhere and have them only look at me. Years later, nothing has changed, only now, I'm more forthcoming about my methods.

"W-what are you doing here?" She freezes and looks down at herself before her cheeks turn crimson.

Fuck me and the way she blushes. No one can fake that, not even Reina's level of conniving manipulation.

I raise an eyebrow. "Did you think I'd ask you to move out if I didn't plan to join?"

"Well, I thought you'd tell me first." She tucks a strand of hair behind her ear as if she's self-aware.

That's what I like about this new version of her—she's more real, human.

Breakable.

This Reina isn't scared of showing her emotions, unlike the old one who did everything to smother them—even if it meant hurting herself and everyone around her to achieve it.

Her world was a constant battle of being a robot, being re-actionless and blank. Maybe that's why she's now having these moments where she just breaks, letting the outside world crack her armor.

This Reina doesn't remember why she needed to hide her emotions, and as a result, she's more genuine.

More…fun.

"I'm here, aren't I?" I ask.

"Well, obviously." She peeks at me through her lashes. "How long do you intend to stay?"

"As long as I please." I have all my stuff in my car and will bring it up later.

I'm not leaving Reina this time. I made that mistake before and she decided to escape. If I had been here beside her or even tormenting her, she wouldn't have thought of that option.

She wouldn't have been attacked by a monster that night.

"Whatever." She huffs. "Can you leave the room?"

"Why?"

"I have to change, dude."

Dude. Seriously, sometimes she's an entirely different person altogether.

My lips twitch in a small smile. "No."

"No?"

"It's not anything I haven't seen before."

She nibbles on her lower lip, her face turning an adorable shade of red. "Fine, I'll change elsewhere."

"That's not how it works, prom queen." I tilt my head to the side. "We have something to settle."

Her brows furrow.

"I gave you two days to move, and they have turned into three."

Apprehension fills her gaze as her breath hitches, no idea whether it's with excitement or fear.

Knowing Reina, it's probably both.

I wasn't sure before, but now I am. "You did it on purpose."

Her only reply is to rub her foot on her other leg's calf.

That's all the answer I need.

"Come here." My order is loud and firm. It works, too, since her movements freeze.

She stares at me with caution, but the spark doesn't disappear as she slowly asks, "Why?"

"When I order, you obey, remember?"

Slowly, she approaches me. The heavy rise and fall of her tits distracts me from everything else until my gaze trails to the demure movements of her toned legs. Those legs were made to wrap around my waist as I thrust in and out of her hot pussy.

She stops in front of me, filling my space with the scent of her shower gel, lilac and something else that's entirely hers.

She's Reina, the only Reina I've ever known.

"Now what?" she whispers, her breathing hitching on the last word.

"Shhh." I lean back on my hands. "Don't talk."

She watches the movement of my hands as if she's a prisoner and they're her wardens. If anything, she appears disappointed I'm not using them.

"Do you want me to touch you, Reina?" My voice drops in range.

She bites on her inner cheek but says nothing.

"Answer me or nothing happens."

"I..." She breaks eye contact and focuses on her toes, which are curled in the plush carpet. When she speaks, her voice is barely audible. "I do."

"I didn't hear that." I soak in her reaction as I continue, "Now, look at me and say it again."

She swallows so hard I hear it as she slowly lifts her head. Her eyelids lower as she says, "I do."

"Too bad you don't deserve it." My gaze trails up her legs, her perky tits, and her damp neck until I reach her face. "You think it's fun to defy me, prom queen?"

"N-no?"

"Why did that come out as a question?"

"I don't know." She's breathing harshly, and judging by the death grip she keeps on her towel, she's turned on but doesn't like to show it.

"Drop the towel."

She sucks in a harsh breath as her gaze meets mine. There are a thousand questions in those blue eyes.

Why are you doing this? Aren't you supposed to hate me?

Just like her, I have no answer, because that's the problem with Reina.

I keep coming back to her whether I like to or not. She has me under some black magic. It's in the way she looks at me like she never looks at anyone else.

Like I'm her one and only.

"This is so fucked up," she murmurs, as if translating my thoughts.

"That we are." I motion at her hand. "Now, drop the towel. I won't repeat myself another time."

I can feel her giving in before I see it. Another thing about this Reina? She lives in the moment no matter what her brain tells her.

She removes her hand, and the towel slides down her body before pooling at her feet.

Fuck me.

I've never liked looking at a naked woman as much as I love watching Reina.

The slender line of her waist, her hips that were made for my hands, her smooth pussy that's begging for my cock inside it.

My gaze trails up. Her nipples harden under my scrutiny, seducing me closer. It's a blasphemy not to touch her when she's right here.

All mine.

Her tits are heavy and ready for my tongue and lips, or better yet, they could use my cock between them as she held them for me.

One day.

I have so many plans for her body. It was made for me. All of it.

I capture her heavy-lidded eyes with mine. Another thing about her that's never changed—whenever she's aroused, Reina barely manages to keep her eyes open.

It's like she's fighting herself to remain in the moment.

"How should I punish you now?"

"P-punish?" Her voice is spooked, but her features say something entirely different.

Excitement, thrill.

She can barely stay still with the building anticipation, fidgeting and curling both hands around each other.

"You defied me. I don't care for being defied. So yes, Reina, you have to be punished."

Her gaze strays ahead for a second as she sucks on the inside of her cheek. Reina always had a fucked-up type of sex appeal that attracted all the motherfuckers in her vicinity. I know because I always fought the urge to rip their eyes out for looking at her.

And yes, I may have beaten some up.

However, she's emanating a different type of sex appeal now. My cock becomes rock fucking hard the more I soak in her uncertainty and subtle innocence.

She notices it when she focuses back on me, and just like that, she drops to her knees between my parted legs.

The view from the top is surreal. Reina, naked and submissive, kneeling between my legs.

I'll never get used to this.

It was unreal the first time she did it, and it still is now.

I hide my sick pleasure as her flustered fingers undo the button of my jeans. It takes her longer than needed in her eagerness and my cock nearly bursts out of its confines every time her long fingers brush over my erection.

She finally manages to grab my dick with both her slender, tiny hands. I groan as she strokes from the bottom to the top.

The thought that she could've done this with another man makes my bloodstream hot red.

She's mine.

Fucking *mine*.

And no one touches her but me.

"What are you doing, Reina?" My voice is hoarser than usual.

"You said you're going to punish me." She licks the crown of my cock, making sure to gather all the pre-cum on her tongue, and I groan like a fucking animal.

This woman is my hell and I'm ready to burn.

"I'm the only man you'll ever get on your knees for, understood?"

"Yes, Ash."

"Repeat that."

Her voice turns sultry. "Yes, Ash."

"Again." I'll never get used to the sound of her submission, of her words.

"Fuck my mouth, Ash."

I nearly empty down her throat then and there.

Goddamn this side of Reina—it's a one-way road to sin, to nothingness.

Who said it's easy to find the right road? If Reina is the wrong one, I'm not leaving this fucking place for eternity.

I grab a fistful of her hair and wrap it around my hand so I have complete control of her. "Open that mouth."

Still clutching my cock, she does as told and parts her lips for me.

"Put me inside."

With one last lick, she slides my dick into her mouth... her hot, wet mouth.

"Now remove your hands. Place them on your thighs. If they move, we'll do this all night, understood?"

She nods around my cock and drops her hands to her thighs. They're so small and delicate and breakable just like her.

Still grabbing her hair, I thrust my hips forward. Her mouth is tiny and doesn't take all of me. I thrust faster, hitting the back of her throat and grunting with the pleasure it brings.

Her eyes widen and tears form at the corners. Her hands rise, probably in an instinctive reaction to push me away.

"What did I say about those hands?"

She drops them back down, her frantic eyes begging for air. She shouldn't have asked me to fuck her mouth if she didn't know what she was in for.

"This is a punishment, remember?" I groan as she nods frantically.

I pull out and she coughs, spluttering. Drool trickles down the side of her mouth and her face reddens, but she parts her lips again, staring up at me with eagerness.

Fuck, this woman.

Her unconditional submissiveness does shit to the dominant side of me. Who'd have thought the tough, no-nonsense Reina would let me take liberties with her this way?

I thrust in again, hitting the back of her throat, suffocating her then giving her room to breathe, only to pump in and out of her again.

Just like she asked, I fuck her mouth.

I own another part of her that was off-limits before.

"Touch yourself," I order.

This was supposed to be a punishment, but I want to see her orgasm face as I empty myself down her throat.

She doesn't even pause to think about it. Reina parts her thighs and plays with her clit, making unintelligible sounds around me.

"Thrust a finger in." My tone gets raspier with each pound into her mouth.

A loud moan escapes her as her hand disappears between her legs, working herself toward an orgasm.

"Add another one," I order.

She complies, her eyes slightly closing with the move. The sounds she makes are enough to make a priest sin.

Reina is fucking temptation incarnate.

"Harder," I groan. "Faster."

Her hand moves in and out of her pussy in a rhythm that nearly matches my own. Then she freezes, eyes drooping as what seems like a full-body shudder takes over her.

There's nothing more beautiful than watching Reina come,

the way her back arches, her tits perk up, and her pink nipples turn as hard as tiny diamonds. Perspiration covers her brows and she looks like a sex goddess as she closes her eyes, head tilting slightly backward.

A sex goddess who's all mine.

As her wave subsides, I pull out my cock and grab her hair hard enough that her eyes flutter open.

"Open that mouth."

Her lips slowly part.

"Show me your tongue."

Her brows furrow, but she does as told. I place the tip of my cock on her tongue and empty myself down her throat. My balls tighten with the force of my release as I enjoy how my cum coats her tongue and lips, how it streaks on the side of her mouth and down her chin.

Mine.

Fucking mine.

Reina never breaks eye contact as I own every inch of her, marking her so no motherfucker comes close to her again.

"Now, swallow. All of it."

She does, even licking her lips to not miss a drop.

My fingers stroke in her hair as she stares up at me with a content expression, the expression of someone so pleased and boneless.

I release her head and pat my lap. "Come here."

Standing on wobbly legs, she climbs up my body without protest and wraps her thighs around my waist.

I lift my shirt up, throw it beside the bed, and kick my jeans down my legs, letting my cock lie against her bare ass.

Her head rests on my shoulder like a tiny child who needs sleep. She must be tired after all the moving and today's practice.

I wrap a hand around her back. I meant to fuck her, but now, as she lies so peacefully in my arms, I want this moment to last longer.

What the fuck?

Her finger trails up my bicep and my tattoo. She's silent for a while, drawing slow patterns over my skin.

"What language is this?" she murmurs, her voice sleepy.

"Arabic."

"What does it mean?"

My peaceful mood from earlier disappears. I can pretend none of it happened, can pretend all of this is fine.

But it's not.

One day, I'll have to wake up and do what I planned all along.

My fists clench by my sides. "Eye for an eye."

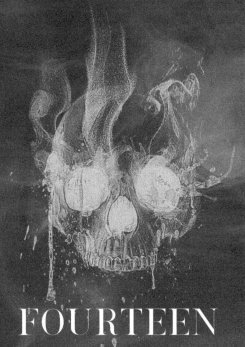

FOURTEEN

Asher

Three years ago

I'm panting as I finish up the asshole who dared touch her.

Put his fucking hands on her.

Made her—

"Fuck!" I roar as I jam my fist into the wall over and over again.

Pain explodes in my knuckles and blood oozes from the cut skin. It does nothing to quell the rage boiling inside me. If anything, it fans the flames, making it burn hotter, needing the release.

I kick the sorry fuck lying on the floor by my feet. He releases a helpless, childlike whimper, but he's already unconscious in the middle of his living room.

When I came here dressed in a ski mask and carrying a bat, I meant to beat him to a pulp, but after the first hit, it just wasn't enough. I had to feel his skin bleeding underneath mine.

Ever since I walked in on this fucker shoving his dick down Reina's throat, all I've been seeing is black.

I punched him at first, and he begged like a damsel in distress. He asked if I'm the father of one of the girls he keeps pictures of. It got interesting then.

I didn't hold back.

I held him against the wall and jammed my fist into his face until one of his eyes swelled shut. His nose is probably broken and he keeps bleeding all over the carpet like a pig.

Then when he fell, screaming at me to spare him, I kicked him some more. When he begged and told me he wouldn't peep on little girls anymore, I pressed on his chest with my boots until I heard the pop of his ribs breaking.

He's out now. Boring fuck.

"Come on." I crouch beside him. "Fight me, motherfucker."

He coughs, gurgling on blood. Both his eyes are now closed, one of them swollen and purple.

I clasp his shirt in my fingers and lift him up off the ground. His blond hair streaked with white strands is half soaked in red.

"You dare touch her." My voice is on the verge of blowing up. "You fucking dare come down her throat."

He murmurs, trying to say something, but it only comes out as unintelligible sounds.

I shake him, making his head loll in an awkward position as if about to snap. When he speaks again, I lean closer to his blood-soaked face, all swollen and unrecognizable.

"S-she…she…b-begged for…my cock."

I freeze, and for a second, I think I'm going to turn to ice and break.

I don't.

A deep, black rage envelops me in its clutches like a vice. I rise to my feet, my muscles clenching so tight as if about to fucking crack.

I kick him in the groin until he wheezes in pain. "This cock?"

He groans and spasms on the floor, but I don't stop. I keep kicking him over and over again until I'm sure I've turned him impotent.

It's a mistake such a sick fucker like him has a working dick anyway.

Once he's no longer moving, I leave his suburban house that he got by teaching kids and getting into their pants.

After making sure no one sees me, I slip out the back entrance and through the bushes where I hid my car.

For a second, I stand there, panting. My hands are smeared in blood, and my shoes are too. I can barely breathe with the ski mask on.

This is what she turned me into.

A fucking criminal with no regrets whatsoever.

She pulled me by the gut years ago and since refused to let me go.

I retrieve my phone and dial the person who'll take care of this whole mess.

"Alexander Carson speaking."

Only my father would answer his son's call by stating his full name.

"Asher Gray Carson speaking." I can't help the sarcasm.

He sighs. "What is it, Asher? I'm busy."

"You'll get busier then."

"What did you do now? Hit another student for looking

at Reina?" He sighs again. "I'm tired of your antics with your classmates. I can't keep paying off those kids' parents every time."

"Sure you can. That's your role, isn't it? Paying for things."

I can imagine him closing his eyes and rubbing his brows. It's what he does every time I tell him he was never a father to Ari or me, as if he's searching for the patience to deal with me.

"Is there a point behind your call, Asher? If not, I have things—"

"I hit a teacher. It's the worst beating so far. I don't know if he'll live or die."

"What did you just say?"

"A teacher, Alexander. I want him gone from Blackwood. Make sure to search his background—he's a fucking pedophile."

"How involved are you?" His voice is strained.

To an outsider, it'd seem as if he cares about his son's wellbeing. In reality, he doesn't want anything to smear his perfect, diligent name, which he spent years building. If his son is labeled a criminal, no one will hire his firm.

I stare at my hands and the blood glinting in the light.

How involved am I?

"Very deeply," I tell Alexander.

"Have you left any fingerprints?"

"A few, yes." I came with gloves, but I had to feel his blood on my skin.

"Fucking hell." He breathes into the phone. "Fine, leave. I'll take care of it."

I hang up without another word. Alexander doesn't

deserve any thanks. After all, he left us alone to fend for each other after Mom's death. The least he can do is pay the price for what we've become.

Me, full of rage and deep-seated pain.

Ari, fragile and sometimes cold.

It takes me fifteen minutes to reach our house and then head to my room. For a moment, I stop in front of the room opposite mine.

Her room.

Since her father's death at the beginning of the year, Reina's been living with us.

With me.

In person, but never in mind.

My fists clench on either side of me as I remember the fucker's words.

She begged for my cock.

He could have been lying. I should believe that, but he was in no state of mind to think of a lie after I beat him nearly to death.

Besides, after all Reina has done, what makes this any different?

I close my eyes to push the thought of her away, but the sucking sounds she made from under that table as he stroked her hair assault my brain. She sounded like a fucking porn start.

I should've killed that motherfucker.

"What...what happened?" Her slightly breathy voice makes my eyes open.

Reina stands at her doorway in her sleeping shorts and top. They mold against her athletic body like a second skin.

A temptress. She's always been such a fucking temptress.

Her eyes that usually hold no emotions widen a little as she takes in my bloodied hands and shoes, my clenched fists and jaw. I bet I'm a sight to behold.

"What's with your hands? Why is there blood?" She approaches me and reaches a hand out as if to touch me before she quickly drops it to her side, realizing who she is and who I am.

Reina doesn't touch me. She doesn't even let me kiss her. The few times I tried, she shut me off so hard, it still draws a black hole in my chest.

But she begged for the teacher's cock.

She lets the other football players flirt with her as if she's single.

As if I don't fucking exist.

"Have you been hitting people again? What is wrong with you?" She folds her arms over her chest, building that invisible wall between us.

I fucking hate it when she does that.

At this time, I have no room to think, let alone act rationally.

The rage that's been plaguing me since the afternoon has mounted and heightened to dangerous levels.

I thought beating that sick fuck would satiate it, but it's made it worse.

Or rather, his words did.

I storm toward Reina and wrap my hand around her throat, my bloodied hand with the busted knuckles. Reina barely flinches as I slam her back against the wall.

"You." My mouth hovers inches away from hers. "You're what's fucking wrong with me, Reina."

Her face reddens—from the lack of air—but she doesn't struggle. She doesn't attempt to push me off her.

A statue.

A cold, lifeless statue.

Why the fuck have I ever thought she could be something else?

I release her with a roar, my tendons ripping with tension. Then I slam my fists on either side of her face, ripping my knuckles even more.

Fresh blood trails down the wall as I pant, staring down at her. She watches me back with eyes so blue, they could drown me.

She doesn't even blink, just stands there.

But for the first time in a long time, a tear slides down her cheek. It's only one single tear, but it creates havoc in her gaze.

For a moment, her eyes fill with a deep sense of sadness, and it guts me. It rips me open and cuts me into pieces.

I don't think when I lower my head and slam my lips to hers, biting them, devouring them. Reina is that forbidden fruit, something that tastes exquisite because it's sin. Her mouth trembles and I take the opening to thrust my tongue inside. I feast on her, on her breaths and the softness. On her taste and even her fucking coldness.

She doesn't kiss me back. Reina never kisses me back, but at least this time, she doesn't push me away, she just lets me kiss the daylights out of her while she stands there, both her hands glued to her side.

Then, as if realizing she shouldn't let this happen, her hands fist and she shoves me an arm's length away. Her chest rises and falls with exertion, matching the rhythm of mine.

"Forget me, Asher," she whispers. "I don't deserve whatever you're doing for me."

"Forget you?" I wrap my hand around her throat again. It doesn't cut her air off this time; it's only firm enough to keep her in place, to feel her pulse and know she's indeed a human, not a robot. "You think that can happen with a snap of a finger? If I could, I would've done it ages ago."

As quickly as her vulnerability showed, she tucks it away again and her cold self comes back to light, like ice that never melts.

"We're toxic," she says. "That's all we are."

"And it's your fault, prom queen. The next time you let anyone touch you, I'll fucking murder them."

"You wouldn't."

"Try me. You keep bringing out my ugly side, and I'm curious to see how far I'll go." I release her with a shove and stalk back to my room.

After I strip, I stand under the cold shower for more than twenty minutes, my cock hard and pulsing.

Every second, I fight the urge to barge into her room and fuck her while choking her. I don't care how, I just have to fuck her, claim her, teach her she's fucking mine.

Knowing Reina, she'll only let me touch her if I rape her.

She'll stay still as I finish like some fucking animal.

I'm not interested in that. I'm not interested in her cold shoulder and stiff attitude. I want her to scream my name, to writhe beneath me as I pound into her.

I want her to want me as much as I want her.

She's been giving me fucking blue balls for years.

Shutting off the water, I wrap a towel around my waist

and exit the bathroom. I bandage my wounds then don basketball shorts and a T-shirt before sitting on the balcony.

The night sky is bright with so many stars.

A long time ago, when we were twelve, I confessed to Reina how much I miss my mom. It was the first time I admitted it after her death.

When I was ten, I became responsible for Ari and myself. Alexander was useless. I had to be an adult too young, and over time, I always wanted to tell someone I missed my mom. That, sometimes, I looked at her picture and blamed her for leaving us with Alexander, and then I felt shitty about it.

The only person who knew that was Reina. It was nighttime and our fathers had some meeting, so we lay on our backs in the backyard and stared up.

Reina pointed at the stars and mentioned her dad said her mom is looking down at her from up there. She said it was stupid and she didn't believe it. She told me I needed to take care of myself so when I meet my mom again, she'll be proud of me.

Then, she held my hand and told me, "I want my mom to be proud of me when we meet again. I miss her, too."

I think that was the moment I got caught in her trap and never managed to find a way out.

Reina wasn't as closed off back then as she is now. She used to talk to me and tell me things. We used to be friends, best friends even.

The change began after our engagement. She started keeping her distance, as if she wasn't supposed to be seen with me.

It's become the worst since Gareth's death. She let me

hug her to sleep on the night of his funeral, just that one night, and in the morning, she turned into this unfeeling statue who acted like a robot.

Who antagonized me on purpose.

Avoided me on purpose.

A deep sigh rips from me as I stare at the stars. Just when did I lose that girl who held my hand? Can I even get her back now?

"Gray!"

My baby sister Ari barges onto the balcony, a wide grin on her face.

Fuck, I've been too preoccupied in my reverie; I didn't notice her coming in.

Ari's black hair is gathered on top of her head as her eyes glint. They're light green and blue, a mixture of Mom's and Alexander's. Her face is so much like Mom, as if she'll grow up to be her one day.

All the excitement vanishes from her face as she focuses on my hands.

Even though they're bandaged, it's clear they're injured.

"Oh my God. What happened, Gray?"

Ari is the only one who calls me by my middle name. It started when we were young and she decided Asher was too hard. Besides, Mom named me Asher after our late grandfather, and Ari wasn't a big fan of him.

"Practice." I grin. "How was my favorite girl's day?"

I don't want to throw my shit on Ari. For her, I'm only supposed to be the brother she can rely on—unlike our father.

"Boring." She sits opposite me. "And that can't be from practice."

"Don't worry about it."

"I'm worried about *you*." She stares at her lap. "You're the only one I have, and I feel like I'm losing you to your obsession with Reina."

I freeze, my chest tightening with tension. Maybe I haven't been discreet enough; maybe my moods are affecting Ari.

Fuck. Her therapist told us not to expose her to too much stress.

"It won't happen anymore." I soften my voice. "I'll be cool."

It's a lie.

This thing won't stop.

Call it an obsession, an addiction, or sheer insanity, but it just won't stop.

It keeps pulsing under my skin like a fucking beast, destructive and deadly.

"I understand why you're like that with her, you know." She peeks at me before she focuses back on her nails, clinking them against one another.

It's her nervous habit.

"Reina is special, but she doesn't love anyone." Her voice fills with sadness. "Not even you, Gray."

My jaw tightens and I force it to loosen up.

Don't affect Ari.

Don't you dare affect Ari.

If she's too stressed, she'll just start doing stupid shit like walking in the night and crying out of nowhere.

We barely got her stabilized, with Reina's help. We can't go back to that phase.

"But you just can't help it, right?" she asks slowly.

"I can."

Her eyes light up. "You can?"

I would do anything to keep Ari happy. Fucking anything.

"Of course. I'm only with her because of Alexander and Gareth's deal. Reina means fuck to me. I never even liked her that much."

"Really?"

"Yes," I lie through my teeth.

Ari needs to believe I'm keeping it together in order for her to follow through. She emulates me in everything, sometimes mood included.

"In that case…" She stares back at her lap. "I have a confession to make. You're the first person I'm telling this, and… and…I-I don't want you to judge me."

She's back to clinking her nails.

I force my gaze away from them and smile. "I'd never do that. I'm your Gray, remember? The cloud that protects you from everything."

The clinking stops as she smiles up at me.

Even her smile is like Mom's.

Soon after, she stares at her lap again. "When Reina came into our lives, she took care of me without asking for anything in return. It made me feel so grateful to have someone else besides you and Dad care for me. I thought…I thought only my family would ever love me, so when Reina did, it brought brightness to my life."

I nod. While Reina changed toward me, she never treated Ari differently. She took care of her and stopped other students from bullying her.

And for that, I'm grateful.

"Over time..." She trails off then blurts, "The brightness intensified."

"Right."

"You don't understand?" She peeks at me.

My brows furrow. "Understand what?"

"I love Rei."

"I know you do."

"No, not that type of love. I'm in love with her, Gray—romantically. Like I can't live without her."

I remain still as if someone spilled a bucket of ice water over my head.

In love with her.

Romantically.

What in the ever-loving fuck?

Ari goes back to clinking her nails manically. "You...you said you wouldn't judge me."

Fuck.

My pulse rises as if I'm coming down from an adrenaline high.

Am I surprised my baby sister prefers girls? Sure, a little, but I'm not judging her for that.

Not at all.

If she thinks she's better with a girl, so be it. It's her life.

But why the fuck does it have to be Reina?

Just why?

"Do you...do you hate me?" Her voice turns brittle. "Please don't hate me. I'm so sorry, Gray. I didn't mean to be like this and..."

"Hey." I take her hands in mine, forcing my face muscles to stop clenching. "I'll never hate you, Ari. You're my baby sister. I'll love you until you're old and gray."

"You're okay with what I just said?"

"Sure," I manage to say. "It's up to Reina to decide."

"You think I should confess?" Her eyes regain some of their brightness.

"Do as you like, Ari."

I just hope Reina will turn her down gently. She usually has a good motherly instinct with her.

And I'm sure Reina won't accept. She's never showed interest in the same sex, and while she resisted me, she wasn't always immune to my touch. I always noticed how her skin heated and her body struggled so she wouldn't melt against mine.

Maybe that's why it pisses me the fuck off that she always pushed me away.

When Ari realizes she has no future with Reina, her infatuation will wither away.

"Thanks, Gray!" She throws her arms around my neck in a hug. "You're the best brother in the world."

No, I'm the worst.

Because I don't want to share Reina.

Not even with my sister.

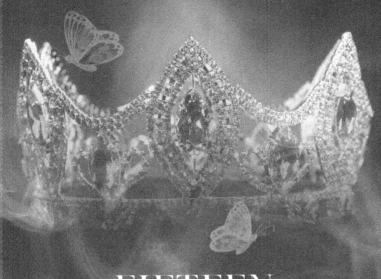

FIFTEEN

Reina

I t's been a week since I moved back into my apartment—or rather, since Asher and I moved in together.

He brought his clothes and laptop and has taken up space in my closet without asking for permission.

Not that I want him to.

Honestly, I don't think I could've done this without him. Being on my own scares me more than I'd like to admit. That's when the gloomy cloud strikes, filling my head with all those somber thoughts.

I listen to Lucy and Prescott's discussion about some moves the coach has added to our routine. They're bickering, and while it's adorable to watch, my mind isn't with them.

It keeps wandering back to Reina. While Alex promised he'll let me know as soon as his insider gets in touch, I'm still antsy.

I have to repeat to myself that Reina is stronger than me.

She survived this long in the midst of monsters. Surely she can keep doing it.

Aside from my sister, something else keeps occupying my mind.

Asher.

He's been acting strange, to say the least.

Every day, he cooks me dinner, nothing fancy, but it's always delicious and he usually feeds me, making me suck his thumb after. Then he joins me in the shower and orders me to take him in my mouth before he empties down my throat or on my breasts.

After that, he carries me to my bedroom in his strong arms and eats me out or finger-fucks me. Other times, our sexual encounters end up in a sixty-nine. Yesterday, he fucked my tits, making me grab them as his length thrust mercilessly between them. While doing that, he ordered me to open my mouth so his cock hit my tongue with every thrust. I can still taste his cum all over my lips as he came with a harsh grunt.

I haven't been as turned on as I was last night in my entire life, so when he fingered me, I came in seconds.

Then…the end. I kid you not, he stopped as soon as I orgasmed, just as he does every night.

Oral sex is the only thing we've done.

Asher has never gone all the way with me or attempted to.

While he sleeps beside me, he always disappears before I wake up, and I find him in the kitchen preparing breakfast.

What is all of that supposed to mean?

He can't possibly not want me, because he gets so hard the moment we're done. He also watches me like he wants to fuck me in the most ruthless way possible, like he wants to choke me and cum inside me.

However, he's not acting on it.

Seriously, if he continues stimulating my body in that unapologetic, wild way, I'll end up begging him to fuck me already.

For some reason, I don't think that'll work with him, though.

Asher has impressive self-restraint, which is all part of his intense dominance. He thrives on control and applies it to himself as well. It's nearly impossible to bust his walls down unless he leaves some sort of opening.

Eye for an eye.

Those words he told me keep bouncing in my head. Revenge, or rather justice. That's what they mean, right?

Whenever I touch his tattoo, he closes off completely. He might still sleep beside me, but he turns stone-cold, like the Asher I met when I first opened my eyes at the hospital.

He's here beside me, but sometimes, he's not. A burst of loneliness hits me whenever he cuts me off and disappears inside his black castle with high towers and metal gates.

My chest constricts at the thought that he might never forgive me.

Every castle has an opening; I just need to search closer to find it.

I need to figure out what he thinks I did and fix it somehow—or at least hope it's fixable.

Because I don't want to have parts of Asher while he keeps the others hidden.

I want the light and the darkness. The sanity and the madness. The beauty and the ugliness.

I want everything.

Just like I need him to accept me whole.

With a smile, I tell Lucy and Prescott to tell me about their decision after lunch, then I leave them alone.

Fine, I might have started helping Prescott in his quest with Lucy. She's obviously interested in him, but she's always backed off, thinking he had eyes for Bree.

Speaking of which, I make my way down the hall. I don't bother with greeting the students who laugh in my face and write nasty comments on that shady Instagram account.

I don't owe them anything. If they don't like me, get in freaking line and stop being hypocrites.

Bree grabs her books, lowering her head. Since she was kicked off the cheerleading squad last week, she's been the latest gossip around campus.

Naomi made it clear Bree's not welcome to sit at our table at lunch, and everyone else on the squad has been steering clear of her.

Blackwood-Black-Book posts about her more than me now.

As soon as she sees me, she glares and brushes past me.

"Do you want your place back?"

She stops in her tracks and turns around as the last of the students trickle outside. It's only her and me now.

"Is this some trick?" she snarls.

"A trade." I face her and cross my arms over my chest.

Asher doesn't like it when I do that, but it doesn't matter when I'm with other people. Besides, I need all my forts to face the enemy.

"What type of trade?" she asks slowly.

"Tell me what I want to know and I'll allow you back in."

She holds her books close to her chest, unable to hide the spark of excitement in her eyes. While a bitch, Bree's a good asset to the squad, and she must've realized now that she's nothing without the cheerleading team backing her up.

"What do you want to know?" she asks.

"Back in high school, when Arianna was alive, what was our actual relationship like? And I'm not talking about what the others think. I need facts."

Whenever I've asked Bree about this, she'd usually back off. I think Asher has told her not to breathe a word about the past to me, or maybe she did it because she's always had eyes for him.

Now, she has no choice but to answer. It's the only way she can leave college life with honor, and someone like Bree would never miss that chance.

When negotiating, always have the upper hand.

Dad's words echo in my head as if he said them yesterday.

"She..." Bree clears her throat. "She was really clingy. There are best friends and there are parasites, and Ari was definitely the latter. She practically sucked the life out of you."

"How so?"

"She was always there, you know. *Always*. Like your fucking shadow. You never had alone time with Asher, and you liked the bitch a bit too much to tell her off."

"Can you talk nice about the dead?"

She lifts a shoulder. "I never liked her, okay? She gave off vibes. I swear I saw her put the bra in Asher's bag that day."

My brows furrow. "What bra?"

"Right, you don't remember. Well, you had a huge fight with Asher senior year after you found a bra in his sports bag."

"And you saw her put it in?"

"I did and I told you but you didn't believe me. So whatever. It's not like I have any reason to lie now." She readjusts her purse over her shoulder. "Besides, it's not a coincidence Asher caught you sucking off the history teacher soon after."

My eyes almost bulge out. "*What?*"

"It was the talk of everyone at school. Asher and I walked in on you sucking off the history teacher. You were hidden under the table, but the teacher was saying things like, 'Yes, more, Reina. You're such a good girl, Reina.' It was like so gross."

No, no. I wouldn't have done that, right?

Even Old Reina wouldn't stoop to that level.

"What did Asher do?"

"What do you think? He walked out. I've never seen him as angry as he was then. I'm sure he's the one who attacked the teacher that weekend and forced him to quit."

My mind reels from the amount of information being thrown my way. How could I do that to him?

Am I really the monster he said I was when I woke up in the hospital?

"As I was saying, that incident and the bra incident were so close. It was really bad between you and Asher."

"Bad how?"

"Super bad, like you could feel the tension in the air whenever you were in the same place. No one knew if you were going to fuck or shoot each other in the head." She lifts a shoulder. "But you always had shitty communication with each other, so whatever."

Shitty communication with each other.

Is this even a case of communication gone wrong? The evidence was all there. I thought he cheated on me, and then he witnessed a disgusting scene.

Please tell me I didn't do it for revenge. Even teenage me wouldn't be that immature, right?

"Then, soon after those incidents, Arianna committed suicide. It killed your relationship once and for all," Bree murmurs. "At least, I thought it did."

This is my ex-best friend saying in no uncertain terms that she always had eyes for Asher.

Well, not on my watch.

An ugly green monster rears his head at the thought of any other woman putting their claws on him.

Hell, I don't think I can even give him back to Reina if she returns and asks for her life back.

How could I stay calm all those years ago after knowing he'd cheated on me?

I shake that thought away and focus on more important things. "How did those incidents relate to Arianna's death?"

"Beats me. All I know is she was a little creep and Asher left you and Blackwood right after her death." She pauses. "Can I get my position back now?"

"Sure. But you're no longer a sub-captain."

"What?" she snaps.

"That position belongs to Prescott and Lucy now. If you're coming back, it's only as a normal cheerleader. Take it or leave it."

"Fine!" She hits my chest on her way out. "You're such an unfeeling bitch, Rei. No wonder Asher left you. Who wants to be with a cold stone like you anyway?"

Her words remain with me even after she stomps out.

No wonder Asher left me.

No wonder he's planning to leave me again.

It's all because of Arianna.

My muscles tense and my heart skips a beat as I rear back from the force of a flashback.

Three years ago

The nerve.

The fucking nerve.

How dare he accuse me of cheating on him when he did it first?

How dare he yell in my face as if I'm wrong and he's always Mr. Right?

I jump backward three consecutive times and land hard on my right leg.

Fuck.

I kick it against the ground. Useless leg. Useless everything.

Flopping down on the chair, I catch my breath and wipe my face with the towel. The outside pool overlooks the backyard where Asher sometimes works out with Owen and Seb.

Not today.

It's not like I want to see him right now. I'm seething and boiling like a fucking kettle.

On the outside, it appears as if I'm practicing, my expression cool and focused. Truth is, I'm blowing off steam so I don't combust.

Practicing is the only way I can do that. When I jump in the air, it's like I embrace complete freedom, the type I'm not allowed on the ground.

People think I don't feel. I wish I didn't. If that were the case, I wouldn't have the urge to jam my foot into a wall then break down in tears.

God, I feel so much like crying.

But I seal that urge in, hardening it with ice.

Mom said crying is for weaklings.

I'm strong, just like my mom, just like Reina, who I hope is also holding on.

After all, she seems to have inherited my mom's genes more than I did. She's the one who ran straight into danger, and I'm the one who left her behind and ran the opposite way.

"Rei." Ari's brittle voice pulls me back from my mind.

Plastering on a smile, I wipe the side of my face and turn toward her. She's wearing one of her long skirts and a blue top.

Her jet black hair, the same color as Asher's, falls on either side of her face in a short cut. Unlike me, she has no makeup on and is watching me with a kind, worried expression.

I tap the chaise lounge beside me, and she trips over her own feet to join me.

She's warm that way, Ari. Sometimes, it seems too warm to be true.

Ever since I've gotten to know her, I've seen a similarity to my relationship with Reina. No one can replace Reina in my heart, but Ari comes close. I've loved her and taken care of her as a sister since we met six years ago.

"I'm so sorry about Asher. He can be so dumb sometimes." She digs her teeth into her lower lip and clinks her thumbnails against each other.

Despite how close we've gotten, Ari has never actually lost her anxiety. Asher told me she developed it after their mother died. Ari saw it as some sort of abandonment and reacted hard to it. Her brother and I silently agreed to protect her from the harsh world surrounding her.

Well, as much agreeing as we can do. Asher and I are just… wrong. I don't know if there'll be a day when we'll be right.

"It's okay," I tell her. "I'm used to it."

"Well, I'm not." She lowers her head. "I'm sorry he doesn't love you."

Her words are like knives shooting straight to my heart. Deep down, I knew it, but to hear it out loud hurts more than I'd like to admit.

It's like bleeding out—silent, but deadly.

Just when did we reach this phase? When did Asher and I stop holding hands and sneaking out to meet each other?

I know when.

When he first kissed me at fourteen. A real kiss, a kiss with sloppy lips and clinking teeth and wandering tongues.

I realized I couldn't possibly live without this boy anymore, and it scared the fuck out of me because Asher isn't mine. He's Reina's. I was only supposed to be friends with him, not decide I want to keep him for my selfish, backstabbing self.

Then Dad and Alex announced the engagement and I made the decision to stay the fuck away, bury my feelings, and pretend I had none.

That was the only way to keep away from someone who didn't belong to me.

"I don't think he has that in him." Ari's bright blue-green eyes meet mine. "He's like my dad. I don't think he ever loved my mom."

Not finding words to say, I nod.

"I-I wish I knew that before," she stammers.

"What do you mean?"

"I...I don't want you to judge me, Rei. You're like the only friend I have."

"It's okay, Ari." I hold her hands in mine. "You can tell me anything."

"You're not going to judge me?"

"Never." I smile. "Best friends don't judge each other."

She bites down on her lower lip so hard, I think she'll draw blood. "I…I love Asher."

"I know that."

"No." She meets my gaze then quickly averts it to stare at her lap. "I'm in love with him, Rei. Not like a sibling, but as a man."

I freeze, my hand turning stone-cold around hers.

Oh, God.

"He doesn't love you," she blurts and goes back to clinking her nails against one another. "And you never loved him, so can you please leave him to me, Rei? You can find better, I know you can."

For a long time, no words come out of my throat. I can't speak or breathe.

I can't do anything.

But as I stare down at her, I see it loud and clear. The pieces start falling together one after another. The miscommunications, the incidents, and the fights make sense now.

I can't believe it took me this long to see it. How could I be so blind to the facts in front of me?

How could I let my emotions lead me?

This has to end. Now.

I need to speak to Asher.

SIXTEEN

Reina

I don't go home that night.

I stay hidden in the locker room and make sure every-one leaves before I go into the gym and jump.

Over and over again.

Adrenaline fills my system as I run and flip backward. I jump and drop down just so I can do it again.

It doesn't help.

No matter how much energy rushes into my veins, it's too little to satiate the deep ache I've been feeling since I had that flashback.

I bend forward, catching my breath. I'm in my shorts and sports bra, my hair up in a tight ponytail.

The gym becomes blurry as I flop down on the floor, chest rising and falling heavily. My temples ache and my stomach rum-bles its displeasure. I might have forgotten to eat today.

I hold my head between my hands as rampant theories

assault me. Arianna, Asher, and I were so much more than what everyone else thinks.

After she told me she was in love with her brother, I figured something out, and I was going to talk to Asher about it, but what was it?

The logical step would be to ask him, but the truth is, I'm scared. My shoulders shake with terror at the thought of talking to him about Ari.

She's his wound, and if I keep snooping around, he might shut me down immediately.

Besides, he thinks I did something to her.

...did I?

In the beginning, I didn't want to believe that, but after that flashback, I'm not sure. My relationship with Arianna was as odd as her feelings for her brother.

And my feelings for him, too.

Because even back then, it was obvious how much Asher meant to me. I was just a pro at hiding it.

How could someone so young carry the weight of the world on their shoulders? The loss of Mom and Reina, then losing Dad, and to top it all off, I had to push away the only person who added color to my life.

I shouldn't have judged Old Reina so hard. She might have acted like a bitch, but she was also dealing with so much.

Add Arianna and it was a freak show.

"Rei-Rei?" Owen's voice pulls me out of my jumbled thoughts. He and Sebastian cross the length of the gym and stand in front of me.

They're wearing their Devils jackets with messenger bags slung over their shoulders, likely meaning they just finished practice.

I check my wristwatch: eight in the evening. Well, hell, I lost track of time.

"What are you doing here?" I ask.

Owen points his thumb at Sebastian. "He always hangs around the cheerleaders like a creep."

"So do you." Seb searches around me. "Is Tsundere here?"

"Her name is Naomi, and she already left." I jump to my feet and grab a towel from the sidelines.

Sebastian couldn't hide his disappointment even if he tried.

"Told you." Owen waggles his brows. "A creep."

"Fuck off," Seb says.

"He's right." I look him up and down. "It's clear you're attracted to her, so why don't you stop the hot-and-cold attitude and step up? She won't wait until she turns old and gray."

"Deep words, Rei-Rei." Owen clutches his chest. "I think I'm going to cry."

I roll my eyes as Seb glares at me.

"Life is short." A raw sense of sadness assaults me. "You never know what will happen tomorrow, so might as well seize today."

I'm such a hypocrite. I was just telling my mind I wouldn't ask Asher about the past, that I'm fine with our relationship the way it is.

I'm not.

I want to feel him more, have him open up to me more, have him hold me more.

Just *more*.

I'll always want more from Asher.

"Have you picked up philosophy?" Owen pokes my side and I squirm away.

"Those weren't your thoughts before." Seb narrows his eyes.

"You never gave Asher the present. You had him run after you until you were both destroyed."

"You motherfucking idiot." Owen hits his friend's shoulder with his. "That's not our story to tell."

"Well, she erased her memories, so she might as well get a wake-up call." Seb steps closer until he's towering over me. "You don't get to preach about the present when you ruined someone's life in the past. Asher was so caught up in you, he always landed himself in trouble, and do you know what you gave him as a reward? A cold shoulder."

I gulp, my palms turning sweaty. Even though I knew that, it stings to hear it out loud. These are Asher's closest friends. They knew him better than anyone else.

"You think that, too?" I ask Owen, my voice low.

He lifts a shoulder. "I don't like getting involved in people's shit, but yeah, you two were like fire and water. You just never mixed, but I guess I liked to think you had your reasons."

"I did," I whisper.

"Have you told him those reasons?" Seb raises an eyebrow. "Because he didn't return to make friends with you. He's become such a stone since high school."

"*Buuuut* he's softening now." Owen grins. "Whatever you're doing to that fucker, keep doing it. We really thought we lost him with Arianna that night."

"When he went to England, it became worse," Sebastian says. "He acted as if he were completely fine when he wasn't."

We thought we lost him with Arianna that night.

Those words keep bouncing in my mind no matter how much I try to keep them away.

You ruined my fucking life, monster.

It's Arianna's death. That's the incident that ruined everything.

I can't run away from the truth anymore. If I want to figure out how to take my relationship with Asher to the next level, I need to fix the past.

For that, I have to find his wound, try to heal it, and hope it's not too late.

Lies won't shield me anymore. The truth is my only option.

Owen pokes my shoulder. "Don't provoke him."

"Yeah, he's a little fuck when provoked," Sebastian says.

"What do you mean?" I stare between the two of them.

"Come on, Rei-Rei." Owen snaps his fingers. "Stay away from Jason Brighton. Asher never liked him."

"Why?"

"He thinks he was pretending to be Arianna's friend." Sebastian's gaze zeroes in on me. "He's shady and always hangs around campus even though he doesn't study here. Never trust anyone who seems too good to be true."

Well, Jason isn't too good to be true. He's Cloud003 and that guy isn't good at all. He still calls me his slut and wants to fuck me. Besides, Owen and Sebastian hate him because he's with the Knights—the Devils' rivals in Blackwood.

"But Asher likes me." Owen waggles his brows with a sly grin and wraps an arm around my shoulder. "How about that BJ?"

"Drop your hand before I fucking cut it off."

The three of us freeze at the low voice coming from the entrance. Asher barges inside, his fists clenched by his sides as his deep green eyes throw daggers in Owen's direction. I don't know why I'm tempted to stand in front of the football player and protect him.

Owen, Seb, and I might not have gotten off on the right foot, but we've grown close over the weeks. I like having them in my life and I'm glad they're there for Asher when he needs a friend.

Only he doesn't seem to consider them friends right now.

If anything, he appears on the verge of slamming his fist into Owen's face and making the threat about his hand come true.

"Drop. It," Asher growls, but his expression remains neutral, emotionless even.

I know better, though. Asher's rage is the type that simmers under the surface. When the volcano finally erupts, it only leaves ashes in its wake.

Sebastian must feel Asher's murderous mood, too, since he smiles in an obvious attempt to defuse the tension. "We were just leaving."

"We were?" Owen seems oblivious, but I'm not sure if it's genuine or just for show.

Seb grabs him by the shoulder and forces him to release me. "Yes, we were."

Owen winks at me. "See you, Rei."

I wave at them, trying—and failing—to ignore the presence standing in front of me.

As they pass him by, Asher stops Owen and whispers something clipped in his ear. I strain to hear what he's saying, but I can't catch it.

Owen's face remains blank for a moment before he laughs. "That's what I'm talking about."

He winks at me again before Sebastian drags him out.

As soon as the door closes behind them, I realize it's only Asher and me now.

My pulse picks up and I fight the urge to fidget. True, I agreed to confront him earlier, but I'm not ready so soon.

I need more time to cultivate my courage.

"What the fuck were you talking about with those two?" Something ticks in his jaw, and I can't help watching him and his face…his handsome, dreamy face.

Is it weird that I like him seething like this? It means he cares, means he's affected. It fills me with a weird type of hope, the belief that maybe, just maybe, it's not too late.

I lift a shoulder. "The usual."

"Define *the usual.*"

"Just stuff, Ash."

He strides toward me and towers over me, his shoulders on the verge of snapping. "What type of stuff, Rai?"

My heart skips a beat at that name. Even though he knows about it, he only ever calls me Reina. It feels both strange and liberating to be called by that name, the name of the child me.

"Why did you call me that?" I whisper.

"Every time you call me Ash, I'll call you Rai. Don't you hate it?"

"I don't hate Rai. It was my name for twelve years, after all, so if you think it's a jab against me, you have it all wrong." I pause, watching him closely. "Do you hate Ash?"

His lips thin into a line but he says nothing.

"Or do you secretly love it and hate that?" I continue, holding my breath.

Somehow, I think that's how Asher feels about me, or at least that's what I'm hoping for.

He ignores my question and motions behind him. "Let's go home."

Home.

My heart flutters at the word. Why the hell does he keep playing my heartstrings today?

I mean, why would he call my apartment *home?* Does he really think of it as one?

When I don't move, he closes in on me.

He'll take me back to the apartment, bring me to orgasm, and then sleep in another room as if I have the plague or something.

It's time I change that.

Today, things will go my way, not his.

I step out of reach and fold my arms over my chest. His sharp glare makes me drop them on either side of me. *Fine.* I can do it without crossing my arms.

After all, Asher has other triggers.

"What makes you think I want to go with you? I was making plans to have drinks with Owen and Bastian."

His face doesn't betray his emotions, but the stiffness of his shoulders does. There's something I've learned about Asher: he's possessive to a fault. After I lost my memories, he tried to hide it, but it's deep in him. I often catch him glaring at the male cheerleaders and any guy who talks to me. Besides, he admitted to wanting to hurt them whenever they touch me.

If I want to get something different out of him, I need to stir up his ugly side.

Luring the lion in his den is dangerous but thrilling.

Sure, I might end up paying a higher price than I bargained for, but if it manages to break the pattern, it's worth it.

"Is that so?" he asks with a lethal undertone.

"Totally. You just ruined my plans, dude."

"Reina," he grunts, as if he's on the verge of blowing.

"What, Ash?" I feign nonchalance.

His hand shoots my way and he wraps it around my upper arm in a deadly grip, making me wince. With a tug from him, I end up flush against his hard chest, rising and falling with his harsh breaths.

My nipples tighten and my bare stomach erupts in tingles with every brush against his T-shirt.

This close, his sandalwood and citrus scent envelops me in a halo, both smothering and liberating.

When he speaks, goosebumps form across my sensitive flesh. "I know what you're doing, prom queen, and you'll regret it."

SEVENTEEN

Reina

Y*ou'll regret it.*

Although those words should scare me, something entirely different courses through my veins.

Yes, fear is still there. It snaps my shoulder blades together and keeps me on my toes. It's the Asher effect; there's no way to tell what he's going to do next when he's in such a mood.

The moment we step into the elevator and it closes on only the two of us, Asher types in the code to my apartment. I never asked him how he got it, but I don't care right now.

He's still silent like on the ride here. My thumb moves up and down the strap of my bag in an absentminded caress as I watch his side profile.

My toes curl in my flats and my heart rate hasn't been able to go down since we left campus.

It's like my body is a flame waiting for oxygen so it burns everything in its wake.

Asher hasn't touched me, though.

Why isn't he touching me?

Wait—are his thoughts different from mine? What does he mean about making me regret it?

My back flattens against the far corner, and a different type of fear claws up my spine. Is this the part where he finishes what he started all those weeks ago?

No. He promised to let me find my sister first.

But why would he keep his promise?

My swallow can be heard in the small space of the elevator. Suddenly, it feels so stuffy. My breathing turns short and choppy, as if his fingers are around my throat, stealing my air supply.

He must notice the change since he cocks his head to the side to watch me. Those green eyes gleam with something sinister and dark. They're like the woods I lost Reina in, sucking me in until there's no way out.

"Ash…" I trail off, not even knowing what I want to say.

Don't hurt me? Let me find my sister first? I'm sorry I developed feelings for you knowing full well you weren't mine?

"Shh." He shakes his head. "Don't talk. I don't want to hear your voice right now."

I gulp down my unsaid words as the elevator dings then opens; the sound is so loud and damning in the silence, a shiver shoots up my spine and over my nape.

Asher steps outside as I stare at the buttons.

I can make a run for it now. Alex's security would drive me to his house and I could spend the night with Izzy, catching up or playing Scrabble or anything that keeps me away from Asher's clutches, basically.

"Come out." He stands in front of the elevator, both his hands shoved in his pockets.

I glance at the buttons once more.

"If you touch those, your punishment will be worse."

I glare at him even as a spark of arousal clenches my thighs.

Am I sick? Why the hell would the word 'punishment' turn me into such a mess?

He raises an eyebrow. "Are you a coward, Reina?"

I narrow my eyes. He's playing me and trying to stir up my competitive streak.

It's working, dammit.

With a huff, I step into the apartment and stand toe to toe with him. I can tell he likes it by the way a spark lights up his features.

Asher enjoys seeing me with no way out but him. In his sick mind, he wants to be the only one who has such a powerful effect on my life.

He's such an asshole sometimes. Okay, most of the time.

"Go to your room," he says.

"Why?"

"Don't talk and don't ask questions."

"Controlling much, Ash?"

"Yes. Now do as you're told. If I do it for you, it won't end well."

The fear from earlier returns, and I swallow down my reaction to his words.

With one last glance at him, I head to my room.

"Remove all your clothes and lie on your stomach on the bed."

I halt in my tracks and my head whirls back. "What?"

"You heard me." Both his voice and posture are calm, composed, as if he planned this all along. "Not one piece of clothing."

"Why would I do that?"

His only reply is a smirk before he strides to the guest room where he keeps some of his stuff.

I'm tempted to follow him and demand answers, but my mind is in too much turmoil for that.

With a shaky breath, I go into my room.

I'm not going to do what he says. He doesn't get to tell me what to do.

Doesn't he, though? His authoritative, controlling ways always have me bending to his will and enjoying it in sick, deranged ways.

My phone vibrates in my bag, and the sudden sound nearly makes me jump. *Shit.* He put me in an overstimulated state without even touching me.

I check my phone and find a text from him.

Asher: Five minutes.

No.

No, no.

This...this is too similar to Old Reina's affair with Cloud003. All too similar.

Maybe Asher read the messages. Maybe he knows about the affair? Is this a punishment for that?

My phone vibrates again and I nearly drop it.

Asher: Four.

I throw the phone and bag on the chair and lift the hem of my T-shirt, yanking it off over my head. My jeans follow next, then my flats.

As I stand in the middle of my room in nothing by my bra and panties, my chest rises and falls with sharp breaths. My legs tremble so hard, I'm surprised my lungs don't give up on me. My hair is still damp from the shower I took back at campus.

The scent of my lilac shampoo becomes tenfold stronger until it's the only thing I can smell.

My phone vibrates on the chair and I jerk before releasing a shaky breath.

Fuck.

This is worse than being in an adrenaline wave. It's like constant stimulation with no way of release.

Asher: One.

Three minutes have passed already?

Cursing under my breath, I unhook my bra and slide my panties down my legs. A tremor possesses my fingers as my underwear joins my clothes on the floor.

I lie on the bed and stare at the ceiling, resisting the urge to pull the covers up and hide my nudity.

Yes, Asher has seen me naked before, but it's the first time he's ordered me ever so bluntly to get nude. And to my fucking dismay, arousal coats my thighs. He hasn't even put his hands on me yet, but I haven't ever felt as turned on as I do right now.

I rub my thighs together to alleviate the tension, but that only makes it worse, more aching, more unreachable.

This is pure torture.

And only Asher can end it.

EIGHTEEN

Reina

The click of the door is deafening in the silence of the room. I refrain from sighing in relief.

But that's wrong. I shouldn't be relieved when I have no idea what he plans to do with me.

After all, this is Asher. Being unpredictable is his modus operandi.

His steps are quiet, but I can almost imagine him stalking in my direction. I don't dare look up or change position. For some reason, I sense that I have to remain this way.

It feels like forever before he finally comes into view.

My lips part.

He's fully naked, too. His sculpted abs are taut and begging for my fingers to run over them, touch them, hug them – and eventually lick them. The V lines create a masculine view down his hips, but not more than what it leads to.

His dick is so thick and long and hard—so hard it's throbbing. God, how did he fit that thing in me?

It takes me a few seconds to focus back on his face. What I find there causes a shudder to crawl between my ribs and settle in my heart.

There's something unintelligible in his gaze, a madness, an unknown.

He reaches out his index finger and flicks it over my nipple. It thickens into a painful tip. His touch is nonchalant, but it creates a war zone in my starving body.

My poor, sensitive body.

A tingle of pleasure dances down my stomach, clenching for more.

"What did I say?" His tone is calm, too calm—too good to be true.

"W-what?" I'm too distracted by his finger to concentrate on words.

"I told you to lie on your stomach, prom queen."

He did.

Oh, God. He did.

Why the hell did I lie on my back instead? At the time, it felt like a normal thing to do, almost as if he told me to.

I move to comply. There's this urge to fix my mistake; no idea why I have it, I just...do.

Asher wraps a hand around my throat, stopping me in my tracks. The tsking sound he makes wraps a different type of noose around me.

"You've screwed up twice today, prom queen. I'll have to remind you how it goes between us."

His hold on my throat tightens, and I grab his hand with

both of mine. My air is about to be cut off and I claw at him to let me go.

God, I enjoy this dynamic between us a bit too much.

"Drop your hands or I'll tie them."

He...can't possibly mean that, right?

When I don't comply, he releases my throat. I gasp for air as he reaches down to the heap of my clothes. I barely have time to focus as he retrieves my bra and yanks both my hands over my head.

"Ash...what are you doing?"

"I told you—don't fight me when it comes to how things work between us." He snaps both my wrists together and secures them to the bedpost over my head.

I lie in front of him, naked and bound. My chest heaves and my breasts ache with the need to be touched, to be used.

Something about this position is so intimate, so exposing, and yet, it's so...right.

It's wrong to feel so right. It's sick and demented.

"Now, about that punishment..." His hand holds my throat hostage again, and this time he straddles my stomach, his knees on either side of me.

From this position, he appears so devastating and godlike, dangerous and thrilling.

"I'm going to fuck your pussy hard and fast until you scream my name, but I won't stop there. Even when you're shaking and begging me to stop, I won't. You know what I'll do next?" He pauses, and I suck in a breath through my quivering lips. "I'm going to fuck your ass and claim every inch of you so when I'm done, you won't dare think about another man, let alone let them touch you."

My breaths turn choppy and shallow as I try to make sense of his words. He…he's going to fuck my ass.

That's supposed to scare me, but my thighs are tightening for an entirely different reason.

"I'll fuck the memory of any other bastard out of you, Reina."

He doesn't need to. Asher is the only man in my memories. I don't need any of the others now that I have him.

"Open your mouth."

"Why?"

"When I give you an order, you obey, prom queen."

Goddamn him and his bossy side, but I'd be lying if I said it didn't affect me. The insides of my legs are coated in a sick type of arousal.

The moment I part my lips, he shoves something black between them. Wait—is that a…butt plug?

"Suck it."

I don't break eye contact as I do that. His authority and the easy way he commands me sparks pleasure over my entire body.

Lapping my tongue around the plastic thing, I make a show of sucking it like I do to his cock. He loves it when I get down on my knees in the shower and take him at the back of my throat.

As he said, he's the only man I'd ever get on my knees for.

Asher's eyes darken and his cock thickens even more between my naked legs, nearly aligning with my slick folds.

"Enough." He grinds his teeth, popping the plug out. "I was going to ease you into it." He grabs the flesh of my thigh, tracing a gentle finger up to my core.

Only there's nothing gentle about the predatory look he's giving me.

His finger slips inside my soaked entrance, and I bite my lower lip.

"But you had to play your games."

Unintelligible whimpers are the only sounds I can make. I want more of that finger, of those hands, of *him*.

I just want all of him, and sometimes, like right now, it scares me.

How is it possible for someone to want another human being without limits? Without thoughts about consequences?

"Do you know what happens when you play games with me?" He removes his fingers from around my neck and slaps my thighs apart.

I cry out, but before I can come down from the surprise, he slaps the side of my ass cheek.

My moan is broken and barely audible.

"I play you back." He slams into me in one vicious go.

My thighs shake and my walls tighten at the intrusion. My back arches off the bed and everything becomes so full of Asher, his thickness, his sandalwood scent mixed with citrus, his force and even his damn games.

Being bound to the bedpost only heightens the sensation of being completely at his mercy—or the lack thereof.

"How many fucking times have I told you not to test me?" His thrusts are sharp and violent, barely giving me space to breathe, let alone think.

He's punishing me and I'm enjoying every stroke of pain, every brutal touch and savage connection.

I love it when he lets go of his cool façade and shows me his true unhinged self.

Because I know he's only like this with me.

"I'm not that high school kid anymore." *Thrust.* "If I see

you flirting with anyone, I won't only beat them." *Thrust.* "I'll fuck you in front of them." *Thrust.* "And make them hear you scream my fucking name."

A fierce wave grips hold of me.

It could be because of the relentless way he pounds into me, his crude words, his arousing promises.

Or all the above.

"Ash…oh, Ash—" I'm cut off when his fingers wrap around my throat.

It's the catalyst I didn't know I needed until it collides against me and I fall.

I just *fall.*

It's hard, fast, and with no landing in sight, but it's not painful. No, it's liberating. It's like having your soul float in the air.

When Asher releases my neck, it's like he forces my pleasure to a screeching halt. I can't believe I became so used to his sick ways, even my ecstasy depends on it.

A thousand shivers dance over my skin as my limbs quiver from the release. Asher's pace slows down a little, but he doesn't come. Hell, he doesn't look like he's close to coming any time soon.

I love that about him. It's like he can't physically release himself until he's tormented me long enough, pounded inside me hard enough, and owned me whole.

He places the plug between us as he thrusts inside me slow and measured then long and unhurried, the pace so similar to—

No.

I won't go there. If I do, I'll start thinking Asher has those types of deep feelings for me, and when I realize he doesn't, it'll only ruin me.

He traces the plug over my soaked folds. The skin is so

sensitive and swollen, the merest friction curls my toes. My nails dig into my palms until I nearly draw blood. The knot at my wrist isn't too tight, but even that rub is about to throw me over the edge.

"You're wet." He runs the object up and down to where his cock is going in and out of me. "Are you wet for me, prom queen?"

I nod once, my back bucking off of the bed. The deep angles of his thrusts are turning me delirious and mindless.

"And you'll only ever be wet for me." He grunts as he thrusts the plug in my ass. There's no prepping, no warning.

I expect it to hurt like a mother, but it fits there fairly…well.

From what I've heard, it's supposed to be painful, but it's kind of pleasurable? I can feel the thin line between his cock and the plug, and my thighs shake harder at the sensation.

I soak in his pace, the deep thrusts and the glistening of perspiration on his chest. His muscles and tendons snap with the glory of his movements. His hands on my hips feel like anchors, big and hard.

As I ease into the rhythm, Asher slips out of me and flips me over so suddenly I shriek as my breasts flatten against the mattress. With my hands tied, I have no choice but to lie on my stomach in the position he asked me to be in before he came to the room.

"Ass in the air and open your legs. Let me see how wet you are for me."

My thighs are still trembling and refusing to come down from the halo, so it takes me a second too long to comply. The fact that he's standing behind me, seeing me this exposed flames my face.

He grabs an ass cheek in his strong hold and the plug

moves a little before he plucks it out. I nearly protest, but he thrusts his middle finger into my pussy. My hyper-stimulated, sensitive pussy.

I thought I couldn't take more foreplay, but a moan slips from my lips anyway.

It's the Asher effect.

He shredded my soul apart and carved himself a cozy place in there.

His cock glides over my slickness and then back to my ass. The back and forth is burning me up and torturing me.

Oh, God.

Why can't he do it already? Is this my punishment?

"Ash…"

Releasing my ass, he leans over so his hot, taut chest covers my entire back then reaches under me and pinches a nipple. The twist is so hard, I cry out in both pleasure and pain.

"What, prom queen?"

I couldn't speak even if I wanted to. The three-edged stimulus of his finger inside me, his cock sliding up and down my wetness, and now his hand nuzzling and twirling my nipples is enough to black me out.

If he doesn't do it right now, I might legit faint on him. There's only so much my body can take. It's like being in a zone where I can't think or do; I can only *feel*.

A zone only Asher can create for me.

"Beg for it." His teeth nibble on my earlobe as he whispers, "Make it convincing."

"I…I…"

"That's not convincing."

"Fuck me, Ash."

"Where?"

"In the ass. Fuck me in the ass." My voice is breathy, and it feels as if I've said those words before.

"That's my girl." He eases himself inside my ass. I catch my breath as he fills me inch by agonizing inch.

"Oooh…" This is…oh wow, it's a lot different than I imagined it would be. It's nearly as fulfilling as him fucking my pussy, if not more.

Another moan rips from my throat as my eyelids lower and I let myself loose. I don't think about the bindings or anything.

The only thing that fills my mind, heart, and soul is him.

Just *him*.

He grips my hips and thrusts another finger inside my pussy until I'm full of him in every way possible

Oh, God. Why does it feel so good?

And how come there's no pain?

He starts moving both in my pussy and ass, and I forget everything—my name included.

Right now, I'm just with this man and I need him to claim me as much as he needs to.

I need to wake up in the morning and see every mark he left on my body and feel whole.

"This ass is made for my dick, just like this pussy." He starts slowly at first, but then his pace picks up. My body jerks off the bed with the power of his thrusts.

My moans cut off over and over again with the force he's handling me with. That's it. That's how it's supposed to go between us.

I come the hardest I have in recent memory, clenching all around his cock and fingers like he said I would. I scream his name over and over again as if it's a salvation—or damnation, depending on how you look at it.

He pounds into me harder and faster. The strength of his thrusts fills me with so many feelings, but most of all, I'm delirious and happy—so damn happy he wants me to the point of madness, to the point of losing all sense of control.

"You're mine," he grunts. "You always were."

"Always," I pant into the mattress.

"Fucking always." He groans as he slips out of me and hot liquid spills over my ass cheeks and my pussy.

I close my eyes, letting him mark me.

Own me.

After all, I'm Asher's queen in public and his slut in private.

My eyes try to open, despite the fatigue rearing on my nerve endings.

Wait...what?

Where did that thought come from?

Before I can analyze that, I give in to the exhaustion and fall asleep, bound, marked, and utterly pleased.

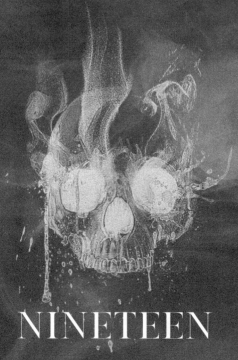

NINETEEN

Asher

She's fast asleep.

I stand there, watching the streaks of my cum covering her ass cheeks and dripping down her pussy and between her thighs.

She's still bound and lying on her stomach, her blond strands sticking to the back of her neck with perspiration. Her cheeks are red and her lips part slightly.

Only one word roars inside me:

Mine.

Mine.

Fucking *mine.*

I'm tempted to let her sleep like that. Worse, I'm tempted to pull up a chair and watch her in that position all night.

Yes, I have a problem when it comes to Reina. Even I admit it.

But she'll catch a cold with the amount of perspiration sticking to her skin.

With one last glance at her, I head to the bathroom, clean up, and go back to the room with a wet towel.

She has turned onto her side, her bound hands lolling in an awkward position. I unclasp the knot and throw the bra onto the pile of clothes. Reina moans when I stroke my fingers over her reddened wrists.

Fuck me.

She looks so fragile right now, I'm tempted to fuck her in all possible positions.

My dick resurrects back to life, agreeing to that idea.

I sit on the mattress and clean my cum off her ass, though I'd prefer it stayed there. But no worries, I'll repeat this—eventually.

With each stroke of the towel against her skin, Reina mumbles something in her sleep. She almost looks like a kid when she's this way, off guard and…innocent.

She always had this certain type of innocence about her that she hid behind her cold exterior. No one managed to come close enough to know the real Reina, let alone her innocent side.

I did.

I'm the one who knows her best, her secret love for mac and cheese, how she stays up late to binge-watch Netflix, how she drinks her lattes, how she hates attention even though it appears she thrives on it.

But where did that leave me?

The memory from three years ago barges back into my head and I curse.

I can't even touch her without being overwhelmed by that

crippling guilt. I can't find pleasure without being shoved into the clutches of pain.

Those who say physical pain is the worst have never experienced being tortured by their own brain.

They've never sat down and felt disgusted with themselves for wanting someone they shouldn't.

"Fuck." I rise to my feet and throw a sheet over Reina's naked body before exiting the room.

I can't stay with her or my brain will eat me alive. It'll feast on my thoughts and leave me a fucking cripple.

For the past week, I thought if I never really fucked her, if I only played around with her, I'd be safe from these dark thoughts.

Turns out, it was useless.

The longer I stayed away, the harder I wanted her, the faster I needed to touch her.

That's how disasters start. First, it's a want, then it becomes determination, and then she challenges me and all I can do is fuck her like an animal. Then like a goddamn lover. Then like she's my slut.

I run a hand through my hair as I toss the towel in the bin.

My phone vibrates on the kitchen counter and I pick it up without checking the name. I need a distraction like I need air.

"Hey, fucker."

An inward groan slips from me as I recognize the British accent and the voice associated with it. I should've checked the name. Aiden King is the last person I need with my current mood.

"Isn't it two in the morning or something in England?" I pace to the balcony, not bothering to put on any clothes. The building across the way is welcome to enjoy the show.

"And?" He sounds bored.

"Sleep, motherfucker—have you heard of it?"

"Sleeping is for neurotypical people."

I should've known he would say something like that. The thing about Aiden is he's proud of what he is, of *who* he is. He knows he's not normal emotion-wise but he embraces it—just like I did after Ari's death. That's why we became sort of friends when I used to study at Oxford. We like the clash of power, the freedom to do whatever we fucking please while sheep follow orders.

"Are you returning any time soon?"

"Why?" I grin. "Miss me?"

"I miss beating you in debates."

"Fuck you. I'm the one who beats your and Cole's asses."

"That's a lie and you know it."

"Is there a point to your call?" I shake my head. "Shouldn't you be cuddling with Elsa and making babies?"

"Don't ever mention my wife's name and making babies in the same sentence or I'll fucking kill you. Deal? Deal."

I shake my head. The asshole is so possessive of his wife, and I always wondered how she took his attitude. Then I returned to Blackwood and realized I'm no different than him.

"Elsa once said she fought you, hard." I flop on the chair in the balcony and cross my legs at the ankles. "How did you overcome that?"

Not that Reina is fighting me right now, but I feel like she'll go back to doing that soon. Every day, I wake up and hold my breath, waiting for the moment she walks out of her room, thinking she'll be the same old cold person.

"Simple," he says. "I didn't give her a choice, especially at the beginning. The more she ran, the faster I chased. The deeper she hid, the harder I conquered."

"What if, after you chase and conquer, she still doesn't want you?"

"Then you're not doing it the right way. Tie her to you and make her see you. If she doesn't like what she sees, make her like it."

"What if she never does?"

"Then you're a fucking loser and probably never deserved her in the first place." He pauses. "As much fun as it's been talking to you, I'm going back to my wife. She's been asking about you, and this is a friendly reminder not to call her. If you do, I'm flying there and cutting out your tongue."

The line goes dead.

Dick.

I'm surprised Elsa asked about me in the first place. She doesn't like me that much, always saying Aiden doesn't need any more deranged friends.

I throw my head back, mulling his words over. It's an interesting angle, the one about never deserving her.

Has that been the trick all along?

I lift my head and stare at the stars. In the blackness of the night, there are a few, but I can almost see a boy and a girl holding each other's hands and grieving together in silence.

Then that image is shattered with no way to be repaired.

Deciding I've given the neighboring building enough of a nude show, I head back inside.

Instead of going to the guest room where I usually sleep, my feet carry me straight to Reina. She's like a fucking magnet, refusing to let me go.

She's still deep asleep on her side. The cover has ridden down her shoulder, exposing the swell of her pale tit.

I don't allow myself to think about it as I slide behind her and wrap a hand around her middle. She's mumbling something in Russian, which means she's probably dreaming about her childhood.

Her brows furrow and her murmurs turn louder. I rub a hand over her cold skin and cover her to the chin. After a few seconds, her lips stop moving and she goes back to sleeping soundly.

I wrap my leg around hers, lay my face near hers, and just like that, I fall asleep.

A nightmare pulls me awake in the middle of the night. I don't remember it, but I don't have to.

Every time I try to ignore the past and sleep with Reina, my brain summons my guilt and makes me relive that nightmarish day.

Reina is still fast asleep in my hold. In the dark, I can only make out the line of her face and neck and feel how her other arm is holding on to mine like it's some sort of a lifeline.

She wiggles her ass against me in her sleep. My already semi-hard dick twitches to life, finding its way between her legs.

I pull her hair to the side, baring her neck, which still smells of lilac and the hint of sex. My lips find her flesh in a feather-light kiss.

A soft moan tears out of her as I suck on the skin. I lift her upper thigh and play with her nipple with the other hand.

"Ash…" she mumbles in her half-sleep.

I slide inside her and she turns her head toward me. Her eyes are closed halfway as she palms my cheek and captures my lips with hers.

It's a soft kiss, slow and passionate. I thrust inside her in the same rhythm, my dick matching my tongue until she shudders and I empty inside her.

I don't bother slipping out of her this time. I need to stay here until I'm able to fuck her again.

A satisfied smile curves her lips as she falls back asleep. I take her one more time during the night, but no matter how much I fuck her, it's never enough.

The more I let myself get lost in her, the harder my brain hits me with guilt.

It's a weird thing, guilt. It's able to eat you from the inside out and you get no chance to fight.

Let her see you.

Aiden's words keep playing in my head most of the night and I find no sleep.

None whatsoever.

At five in the morning, I give up and decide to do something about it.

This has been long overdue.

After putting on shorts, I return to Reina and nudge her shoulder. "Wake up."

She mumbles something but doesn't comply.

"Reina."

"I'm so sore, Ash." She covers her head with the sheet. "Later, okay?"

She must be exhausted from how many times I took her in one night, but this can't wait.

Not anymore.

I fling the sheet from her head. "Wake up *now*."

Her eyes remain closed as she grumbles, "Do something about your stamina, dude."

My lips twitch in a smile before I school my features. "Are you going to wake up or should I pour water on you?"

She sits up like a robot, slowly opening her eyes and wincing. "Ouch, I can barely sit. I think you broke me."

"Come on."

She points at the neon numbers on the clock, expression incredulous. "It's five in the morning. What the hell?"

"Move that ass, Reina."

She glares at me with half-opened eyes. "The one you broke?"

Who knew she could be such a drama queen when she's sleepy and sore.

When I continue staring, she groans, "Fine, coming, coming." She pauses and wraps the sheet around her tits protectively. "Not that type of coming. Don't even think about it, Ash. I mean it."

Fuck me.

I love this side of her a bit too much. That's why a part of me wants to run her a bath and take care of her. It's the same part that fell in love with her a long time ago and doesn't want me to fucking do what I've planned.

But that part has had no say in anything since three years ago.

Reina murdered that part in cold blood.

I grab her by the arm and lift her in my arms, sheet and all. She squeals before her hands wind around my neck.

"Give a girl a warning." She pants as I step into the balcony. "Where are we going?"

I place her on the chair near the edge—the same edge she threatened to jump from not so long ago.

Reina's eyes widen as if she's coming to a realization. She pulls her knees to her chest and visible goosebumps cover her bare shoulders and arms.

She gulps while staring up at me.

Even I don't know how I look right now. All I know is this ends today.

Every. Fucking. Thing.

Just like everything ended three years ago.

TWENTY

Asher

Three years ago

I take two steps at a time toward the school's rooftop. Ari likes to meet here because it's away from other students.

She has a weird relationship with people. Some days, she wants their acceptance. Other days, she just wants them dead.

It's how her brain works, her shrink told us. *You just have to adapt to her and try not to antagonize her.*

My head is still fucking mush after her revelation yesterday. I saw her talking to Reina near the pool in the morning, and that's probably why I'm tense. Or it could be because I'm still damn pissed about Reina and that cocksucker.

And yes, Alexander took care of him. The school got word today that he's moving states, or probably countries. Alexander has a knack for dealing with people and making them disappear.

It's what he does best beneath all the legal talk and the sharp suit.

Then, there's Reina.

Fucking Reina and her cold shoulder and stiff attitude. One day, I'm going to fuck it out of her.

One fucking day.

I jam my still bandaged fist into the wall to release the energy. I can't talk to Ari when I'm in such a volatile mood. She'll sense it and let it affect her.

Opening the door, I stand there for a second and inhale a deep breath. The afternoon sun has turned orange in the distance. It's weird for Ari to stay at school this late, especially since she doesn't have any club activities to attend.

I find her sitting at the edge with Jason. My nostrils flare upon seeing him.

I don't like that motherfucker.

Not only is he hanging around my sister, he's also trying to get his goddamn claws in Reina.

The only reason I haven't rearranged his face and had Alexander relocate him to a third world country is because of Elizabeth.

Upon noticing me, he throws one last glance at Ari. She nods once, and he stands up and heads to the exit. He doesn't make eye contact as he pushes through the door.

"Ari." I try to hold on to my patience as I stride to her. "I told you not to hang around him. There's something weird about—"

I freeze in place when Ari stands up abruptly. Her feet hang on the edge—the literal fucking edge.

Tears streak her pale cheeks, eyes bloodshot and red. Her

white dress and black hair fly in the air behind her. The wind is so strong, it shakes her tiny body.

"Ari...what are you doing?" I try to keep my voice level, try not to freak the fuck out.

I approach her slowly.

"Stop." She holds up both her hands and I stop, my heart beating so loud I barely hear the whistle of the wind or her loud sniffles.

"Ari. Come down, baby sis. We can talk about this, okay?"

She shakes her head frantically. Her leg slips off the edge and I swear my own heart slips out of place as well.

"It's over, Gray." Her voice is so emotional, it guts me.

"Nothing is over, Ari." I reach a hand out. "Come here. We'll work it out, okay? Just you and me."

Her bottom lip trembles as she stares between my hand and the ledge.

The school is five stories high; if she falls, she'll fucking die.

"Don't look there, Ari." I try to approach her but halt when she glares at me. "Come to me, please. Whatever it is, I'll fix it. I'll fix it all."

Ari's had gloomy moods before and often asked me what the point of life is when she was younger, but she never once attempted to take her life.

Not once.

This must be on a different level than anything else that has happened to her before.

"I'm so sorry, Gray. I can't do this anymore."

"Ari, let me help you, *please*."

Her teeth chatter. "You'll help me?"

"Absolutely. I'll help you with anything."

"But you can't change a person's heart, Gray." Fresh tears

well in her big eyes and fall down her cheeks. "I…I told Reina I loved her. You know what she said?"

Fuck. Fuck!

"Come here and tell me, Ari, okay?"

She shakes her head, her leg pushing back. I freeze an arm's length away from her.

"She laughed, Gray." A sob rattles in the air as tears fall down her neck and soak the hem of her dress. "She laughed at me and asked if I was serious. She said my brother and I are so fucking delusional and made fun of me. Why did she make fun of me?"

Reina did that?

Fucking hell. That's the speech she reserves for her haters, not for Ari.

When this is over, I'm going to deal with her. She of all people knows how fragile Ari is. She should've rejected her softly, not been a bitch about it.

"I'll talk to her," I tell Ari. "We'll fix this."

"Don't lie to me, Gray!" she yells, her neck straining with tension. "You can't fix it. You're fucking in love with her. I can see it in your eyes no matter how much you try to hide it. How do you expect me to live with someone who made fun of my feelings while my brother is in love with her?"

"I…" I clear my throat. "I won't be anymore. I promise, Ari. I fucking promise, so come down."

"Really?" She sniffles. "You'll really hate her?"

"I will. Anything for you, Ari."

I'll cut my heart to pieces and stomp on it if I get to keep Ari. She's the only thing I have, the only person I can call family.

I did everything to take care of her. If I lose her after Mom, I don't know what will be left of my life.

She's so young and deserves another chance at life.

She deserves the world.

"Anything?" she asks hopefully.

I give a sharp nod.

"Then don't forget this, Gray." Her face turns stone-cold as the tears and sniffles and sobbing disappear. "Make Reina pay for my death."

And then she opens her arms wide and jumps backward, her dress flying behind her.

"Nooooo!" I roar as I close my hands, but all I catch is air.

I run to the edge, staring down.

The world pauses then.

Everything fucking disappears as I'm slowly gutted by the sight below.

Ari lies on the ground, her head smashed, blood flowing beside her and down her white dress as her vacant eyes stare at nothing.

A roar rips from me as I drop to my knees. "Noooo."

As I kneel there, I realize something.

Ari isn't the only one who died. Today, I died with her.

TWENTY-ONE

Reina
Present

I'm trembling, my limbs, my fingers, and even my lips.

Silent tears stream down my cheeks as I listen to Asher's retelling of Arianna's death.

He's been standing in front of me the entire time, but he hasn't once looked at me, as if I'm invisible.

As if I don't exist.

His entire attention is on the edge where I stood and threatened to throw myself off not long ago. It's like he can see his sister, as if she's still there and he can catch her.

Or at least I assume that from the way his hands clench and unclench on either side of him.

His bare chest muscles contract, rippling and never once relaxing. My hands itch to reach out for him, to hold him, to tell him it wasn't his fault.

But that'll only backfire.

No wonder he's hated me all this time. No wonder he planned to kill me. Arianna and her destructive lies have turned him into a killing machine, a hollow existence without a heart or a core.

That doesn't mean what he did to me is acceptable, but I can't leave him drowning with no way out.

Asher might have held a grudge against me all this time, but I don't think I ever felt any hate toward him.

If anything, my feelings have only intensified, turning hotter, brighter, and scarier.

And for that, I need to fix his misconceptions, even though it'll destroy everything he knew about his sister, the person he considered his only family.

"Do you see now? Do you see how you fucking ended mine and my sister's lives?" He speaks low and threatening, almost like he's on the verge of acting on his destructive emotions.

That's the thing about Asher. Since Arianna's death, he's only survived on the thought that one day he'll bring her justice by eliminating me.

But he hasn't.

For three years, he hasn't managed to act on his promise.

"Why haven't you killed me yet?" I murmur.

"Death is too lenient for you." He glares down at me so harshly I feel it to my bones. "You have to suffer."

"I think I've suffered enough." I keep my voice neutral. "Why don't you kill me?"

He reaches me in two long strides and wraps a hand around my throat. His squeeze isn't threatening or erotic. This one is meant to suffocate, to kill, like in that classroom when I lay on the ground.

Even though my body revolts, begging for life, I don't fight him. I just look up at him as my lungs burn with the need for air.

I don't mean to, but a tear falls down my cheek and onto his hand.

"Fuck!" He releases me with a shove. "Don't fucking tempt me, Reina. I'm this close to killing us both."

I massage my neck, wheezing for breath. A small part of me is rejoicing at the fact that he didn't kill me.

He *can't*.

I can see that torment in his eyes; it's as clear as the feelings I have for him.

"Why both of us?" I whisper. "You only need to kill me."

"Shut the fuck up, Reina."

"Why?" I cry. "Just why? Because you don't hate me as much as you tell yourself? You can't hate me? You want to be with me?"

He crouches in front of me and traps my jaw between his thumb and forefinger. "Because I can't fucking live without you. I tried it and it was hell."

"But Arianna…"

He closes his eyes for a brief second. "That doesn't mean I stopped hating you."

"Then you hated me for the wrong reasons." I swallow. "I think we've been both played."

"Played?"

"I remember the day Arianna talked to me." His jaw clenches but I stop him with a hand on his arm. "Let me finish."

I go on and tell him what Arianna told me about her

feelings for Asher and how she asked me to leave him so she could have him.

For a second, Asher watches me intently, his fingers still clutching my chin as if he needs the connection as much as I do.

Before he can say anything, I blurt, "I didn't make up the memory. Dr. Anderson said it's not possible."

"I know." His voice is quiet, pained even.

"You...do?"

"Yeah, I speak to your doctors."

He does? How come I didn't know that?

"Besides," he continues, "that's similar to how Ari told me she loved you the night before. Fuck."

"Was she...mentally unwell?"

"Yes, depression mostly, but she had that type of behavior, the lying and scheming, but why the fuck would she kill herself if she made it all up?"

"I don't know, but I don't think either of us had the full gist of her state of mind. I think she had more problems than depression. She might have been a pathological liar and well, something else."

"Something else like what?"

"It takes so much to plot all that. It was just a pure masterminded plan to keep us apart."

His eyes rage. "You think my sister killed herself just to keep us apart?"

"I know this pains you, Ash." My palm cradles his cheek as if the touch will take the torment away. "But you have to keep an open mind if you want to learn the truth. It's clear she relied on our lack of communication, knowing full well we'd never sit down and talk about this. From what I've learned, we did have communication problems, right?"

"And whose fucking fault was that, Reina?"

"Fine, it was mine, but you didn't help either." I pause. "I tried to talk to you, right? After I figured things out, I remember thinking I'd talk to you."

He's silent for a bit. "After Ari's funeral, yes."

"And what was your reply?"

He remains silent.

"What did you tell me?" I insist. "And don't lie to me."

He sighs. "The exact words were, *You're fucking dead to me. Don't let me see your face again.*"

His words stab me deep and hard even though I don't remember them. They must've hurt a lot more back then.

Maybe that's why I pulled back and preferred to take his cold shoulder instead of having him hate his dead sister.

Old Reina sacrificed too, maybe too much, even.

I drop my hand from his cheek and try to turn away but he holds my face hostage, making me look at him. "That was right after Ari's death," he repeats slowly. "All I could dream about were her last words."

It's his indirect apology, but it's not enough. I might have had something to do with the way we are, but Asher never fought for me.

Not even once.

Yes, he beat people for me, but he never stood up for me or *with* me.

I guess that was all I needed from him. If he'd done it back then, if he hadn't been too proud to stalk away every time I pushed him, maybe none of this would've happened.

But it doesn't matter now.

"If we're going to investigate this, I'll do things you might not like."

He narrows his eyes. "Such as?"

"Jason. He could be our only bridge to the other Arianna we didn't know."

My fingers shake at the thought. Jason is also Cloud003. He befriended me, fucked me, and was there for me in the most convenient times.

He was also there right before Arianna killed herself.

It can't be a coincidence, right?

TWENTY-TWO

Reina

At night, I go back to Alex's house for a visit.

Asher didn't like the idea that I'd be talking to Jason, and he's been grumpy during the entire ride.

I like watching him be pissy about this; it's better than seeing him broken from the inside out like this morning. Finding out all that about Arianna must've crushed him.

If roles were switched and Reina did that to me, it would've destroyed me, too.

Asher is too proud and stubborn to accept comfort. After the morning confrontation, we went to college, and I'm glad for that. I wouldn't have the slightest clue how to deal with him in that state. All I want to do is hug him, and I know he wouldn't accept it.

Not only is he proud and stubborn, he's also sealing himself off from me.

Still, I want to feel close to him in some way, and I'm ready to take the risk of striking up that conversation.

We cut the distance toward Alex's house in Asher's Mustang. It's quiet and nearly asphyxiating in here.

For a second, I watch the dominance he exudes as he grips the wheel with easy control—like he does with my body.

I briefly close my eyes in remembrance. My ass and pussy are still sore from the powerful way he thrust inside me. He claimed me. There's no way around it, and now, I'll always want more.

Before that, there's something more potent hanging between us that I should try to clear up.

Chasing the remnants of arousal away, I face him, playing with the strap of my bag. "Why did you quit football?"

Asher throws me a brief glance before he focuses back on the road. Since he's been in a pissy mood, I expect him not to answer, but then he says, "It didn't interest me in the long run."

"And law does?"

"Yes, international, not domestic. There's something liberating about moving freely between borders."

Interesting. I thought he chose law to spite his father in some way, but it seems his and Alex's visions are entirely different—even if they have a few things in common.

"Then why did you come back?" I lower my head.

"I told you, it's for you." He shakes his head. "I could've studied here, but I left because of you then I returned for the same reason. I hated you so much, you consumed me."

His quiet confessions are like fire arrows shooting at my chest, burning me alive.

Hated.

He didn't say he hates me; he worded it in the past tense.

Besides, he said I consumed him, maybe as hard as he consumed me. Maybe his hate has transformed into something else now, or is that too much to ask for?

It's funny how I've become careful with how much I can hope for. Now, I'm always scared that if I get too ahead of myself, everything will crumble all around me.

Instead of confronting him about what he said, I choose to keep the hope and ask, "How was your life there? In England, I mean."

"Just a life."

"Can you elaborate?"

He's quiet for a beat. "I had friends, Aiden and Cole. They're a bit eccentric and they managed to keep my mind off things."

They must be the ones I saw in that Instagram picture Lucy showed me. I want to meet them one day, see how Asher lived without me.

"What type of things?" I ask.

"Like coming back and fucking you—those types of things, Reina."

My cheeks heat, and I swallow back the impulse to say *Then why didn't you?*

"How about you?" He pulls me out from my thoughts.

"What about me?"

"How was life for you?" He pauses. "Forget it, you don't remember—"

"Lonely," I cut him off.

His green gaze slides in my direction as if he didn't expect me to say that.

Now that I've started, I can't stop the flow of words. "I might not remember everything, but I clearly remember the loneliness and the fear about the possibility of never finding my sister. Those feelings ate at me from the inside out, but I had to keep up the façade everyone expects of me."

"Not me." His voice is low, deep, and so raw I feel it to my soul. "I like it better when you're natural and uncut. Those masks will suffocate you one day. They're not you."

I fight the pull of tears as I gawk at him. How long have I waited for someone to tell me those exact words? Hell, how long have I waited for him to say anything similar to that?

"How do you know it's not me?" I couldn't speak louder even if I wanted to.

"I just do, Reina. I know you."

And I know you.

But I don't say that out loud. If I do, I'll turn into an emotional mess and demand he cuddles me or something. We don't have time for that under the circumstances.

The Mustang comes to a slow stop in the driveway. I retrieve my bag and step out of the car. As soon as the outside air assaults me, I stop in my tracks.

Detective Daniels.

He stands in front of a police car talking to one of the staff, Joe, who probably wouldn't let him in.

Asher gets out and curses under his breath. "Get back in the car."

You know what? I've had enough. That detective doesn't scare me. The thought of never finding my sister does.

"No," I tell Asher.

Slinging my bag over my shoulder, I stride toward him, my entire body tightening as if hardening for the imminent battle.

"Miss Reina." Joe seems taken aback at my appearance.

"Hey, Joe." I greet him then focus on the detective. "Is there a reason for your visit?"

He narrows his eyes on me for a brief second before he masks his reaction. "Miss Ellis, I was hoping to talk to you."

"Then talk. I'm all ears."

"Have you recalled anything about what happened to you that night?" He retrieves the picture and the bracelet, shoving them in my face. "I'll drag you into court with this and the DNA."

I resist the urge to snatch the bracelet away. It's the only memory I have from my mom and the only thing I kept as Rai. "Apparently, you couldn't do anything with those. I'm going to have my lawyers retrieve my belongings."

He pushes off the car and Joe stands his ground beside me. I don't push back or cower. It was stupid to be scared of him in the beginning, or maybe it wasn't him I was scared of; it was the unknown and the thought that I hurt someone. Now that I remember my meeting with Reina and know full well both of us were victims, Detective Daniels can't do shit to me.

We stand toe to toe. He's taller so I have to stare up at him, but that doesn't reduce my defiant stare.

"You think I'll give up, you spoiled little girl?"

"Oh, I'm sure you won't, and I'll enjoy watching you fail." I cross my arms over my chest. "Now, where's my ring?"

"Your ring?"

His brows scrunch as if he doesn't know what I'm talking about.

I motion at the picture. "I wore my engagement ring that night—where is it?"

"We found no ring."

My heart flutters as I whisper, "So she took it."

Oh, God.

Reina was trying on my engagement ring and it was a bit

loose on her finger, so if she really was hurt or fell unconscious, the ring would've slipped off.

Or that's what I want to believe.

I need to think she kept it because it was precious enough not to throw away.

"She took it?" The detective's eyes zero in on me like a hawk's. "Who is she?"

Shit.

I didn't mean to say that bit of information aloud.

A larger than life presence stops behind me. His warmth envelops me like a cocoon. I don't even have to look back to know who it is.

"If you're done, leave," Asher tells the detective in a firm voice that's too similar to Alex's lawyer tone.

"We're not done." Something glints in the detective's eyes. "Miss Ellis here was just telling me about a *she*."

"That would be the housekeeper." Asher wraps an arm around my waist, and it feels more protective than anything he's ever done before. "Now, leave before I call the other cops on you, the ones who can suspend you."

Detective Daniels spits on the ground before he yanks the door of his police car open and slides inside. He stares at me through the window for a second too long. "I'll get you one day, Miss Ellis."

And then, his car revs up and he drives away.

"Motherfucker." Asher's rage-induced voice prickles my skin.

"I'm sorry, sir." Joe slightly bows his head. "The guard at the gate is new. He didn't know we don't allow the police in."

"It's okay, Joe." I smile at him.

Besides, even my security members aren't allowed to mingle

with the police. After all, they're a legitimate business and can be targeted by the authorities if they make enemies with them.

As soon as Joe disappears inside, Asher spins me around so his arms are surrounding my waist from the front.

His expression is tight and on the verge of hell breaking loose. "Why the fuck were you talking to him? He's after you, and he's not someone to be trusted."

"You think I trust him?"

"Then don't talk to him."

"I won't let him walk all over me or force me into hiding. I did nothing wrong, Ash."

He sighs with resignation. He's started to do that every time I call him Ash now. I'm obviously not going to change the way I address him, so he has no choice but to cope with it.

"You have to be careful, for fuck's sake." He runs a hand through his jet-black hair. "You keep attracting danger like a magnet. I don't even know what the fuck to do with you anymore."

The urge I've been resisting since the morning overwhelms me now. I can't stop it, even if I want to.

My nails dig into his leather jacket and I pull him down as I rise up on my tiptoes. My lips meet his and I plant the kiss I've wanted to give him since this morning.

It's a comforting one, thankful, and everything in between. The fact that he's worried about me makes me fly out of my skin. It's like being high on a dopamine rush with no intention of ever coming down.

Asher groans as his strong hand wraps around the small of my back and he slams me against his pelvis.

My soft, slow kiss comes to a halt, and it's Asher's turn to claim me, devour me, almost like he did in the middle of the night when he woke me up to have sex.

I love it when he kisses me like he's been starving for me, like he can't survive without kissing me.

Asher and I should have been kissing for years.

Why did we take so long to do something so natural?

The clearing of a throat makes me jerk back from his mouth. Asher doesn't let me go, though, his arm remaining like a cage around my waist.

I forgot we were outside and that Alex could see us. *Shit.* Just because he's been keeping quiet about the fact that Asher and I live together doesn't mean I should give him any ideas.

The one who interrupted us isn't Alex, though. Jason stands beside his truck, appearing a bit awkward.

I place both palms on Asher's shoulders and whisper so only he can hear me. "Let me go."

"Why?" That intense possessive look returns. "You're my fiancée, remember?"

"Ash."

"Stop acting like you're not mine or I'll prove it right here, right now."

I gasp, staring at him with incredulity. If I think that's an empty threat then I'm only fooling myself. He's crazy enough to do it, damn him.

"Fine, I won't." I lower my voice. "Let me go and I'll do something to prove it."

He narrows his eyes as if not believing me.

"Trust me."

I don't expect him to, since he's never shown a sign of ever doing that, but he slowly lets me go. For a moment, I'm stunned into silence. Does that mean he does trust me?

No, no, brain. Don't you dare have any high hopes.

As soon as Asher's arm falls from my back, I slip my hand into his, threading our fingers together.

He stares at my expression then at our linked hands with slight awe on his face.

"I guess I never did this before either?" I ask.

"You did." He appears nostalgic as he strokes the back of my hand with his thumb. "When we were thirteen."

"But not after?"

He shakes his head once.

Damn you, Old Reina.

I pull myself out of that trance and focus on the now. "Let me talk to Jason alone."

The slight improvement of his mood vanishes, and his hold tightens around my hand. "Fuck. No."

"Hear me out."

"No, and that's final. There's no fucking way I'm leaving you alone with him."

This isn't the time for his jealous possessive episodes, dammit. "We're friends, Ash. You're not. Jason will be more comfortable talking to me alone."

"We'll do it together or not at all."

"You're so fucking stubborn, do you know that?" I glare up at him.

"Not as much as you."

With that, we both head over to Jason, who has been watching our interaction closely.

"Hey, Reina." He smiles, his gaze flitting to Asher's fingers in mine.

"Hey, Jason." I smile back, trying to dissipate the tension floating in the air. "I was hoping we could talk to you?"

"We?" He appears wary as he glances between me and the tension ball by my side.

"Yes, *we*," Asher says with a calm he sure as hell doesn't feel. "Do you have a problem with that?"

"No." Jason pauses. "It's just that I have nothing to talk about with you."

That's not good. If Jason means that, he won't divulge anything in Asher's presence.

"When it comes to whatever relationship you had with my sister, yes, you do."

I dig my nails into Asher's skin, trying to shut him up. I'm sure he sees the way Jason has straightened. He hit a nerve, and if he doesn't back off right now, we'll lose our only thread to the truth.

"I don't know what you're talking about." Jason maintains his cool façade.

"What did Ari tell you that day?" Asher's threatening aura might as well have turned into smoke and be looming over us.

"She just told me to take care."

Asher steps forward and I know he's about to grab Jason, or worse, smash his fist into his face. He's provoking him, and Asher has been volatile since the morning. It's almost similar to the resurfacing of the old Asher with his quick fist and ever-changing moods.

I grab his arm with my free hand and say, "Do you know anything else? Something that could help us in uncovering the reason behind her death?"

Jason lifts a shoulder. "No, not really."

He's lying.

Even though there are no obvious tells, I can sense he's hiding something. As I predicted, he'll never say it in front of Asher.

Jason smiles at me. "If you need anything, you know where to find me."

And with that, he gets into his truck and leaves the mansion.

A sigh tears out of me as I face Asher. "Happy now?"

"Why would I be happy?"

"You just ruined it. I could've gotten some answers if you'd let me talk to him alone."

"That won't happen, and it's final."

Ugh!

I remove my hand from his. "I'm going to say hi to Izzy and Alex."

Two steps are all it takes before he grabs my arm and pulls me back. I gasp as I trip and nearly fall. Asher straightens me and grips me by the chin, forcing me to stare at those bottomless green eyes.

They've been gloomy like a forest under bleak weather today, and while I want to comfort him, his stubbornness is making me rage right now.

"Did you just snap at me?" he asks with a dangerous tone.

"Yes, I did! You're infuriating. I don't even know why I…" *…keep loving you so much.*

Damn. I almost said those words out loud.

What scares me more is how much those words are true, how much I really love him, have always loved him, and how much it hurt to be away from him and know he was never mine in the first place.

I guess I only came to terms with that fact after I lost my memories and gained some sort of freedom.

God, I love him.

I'm *in love* with him.

I have never felt as attuned to a person as I am to Asher. My orbit keeps turning around him, or rather, I keep floating in *his* orbit.

Although I don't remember everything about the past, I remember my connection with him. Maybe that's why it was so easy to let go after I lost my memories.

"Why you what?" He watches me intently, as if he can crack open my skull and peek into my thoughts.

"Nothing." I wiggle free. "I'm going to see Izzy."

If I stay with him one more minute, I might actually say the words out loud and put us both in a position neither of us can afford to be in.

I'll deal with all these emotions later.

After I find my sister and uncover the truth about Arianna's death.

Because what I feel for Asher is too raw and deep to be resolved so easily.

He doesn't stop me this time, and I'm thankful for it.

Izzy greets me at the entrance, her face ashen. She keeps wiping her dry, clean hands on her apron over and over again. Upon seeing me, she reaches into her pocket then quickly shakes her head.

Has she been there all along? Did she see the exchange we had with Jason?

"Hey, Izzy." I lean in for a hug and she returns it with a stiff smile.

Once we break apart, I notice she's still watching Asher, who headed back to his car. No surprise there. He has no interest in seeing Alex, and now that he made sure Jason isn't in the house, he'll remain in the car until I come out. After all, he only dropped by to be with me—and ward off any one-on-one time with Jason.

"Is Alex here?" I ask as I walk inside.

"Yes...uh...he's in his office."

"Thanks, Izzy." I smile, unsure why she's in a jerky mood. "Are you okay?"

"Me?" She nearly yells then stops in her tracks by the stairs. Sweat beads on her forehead and she keeps wiping her hands on the apron.

"If there's something going on, you can tell me." I face her, softening my voice. "I'll do whatever I can to help. You've done so much for me since I woke up with no memories, and I'll never forget that."

A sudden sob tears from her throat and my eyes widen. It's the first time I've seen Izzy out of sorts like this. She is always the epitome of care and kindness.

"Izzy." I clutch her shoulder. "Please tell me. I want to help."

"Why did you have to be like this?" She sniffles. "It would've been so much easier if you were the old Reina. Ever since I found this, I can't sleep."

"Found what?"

"Even though I would give my life for him, I can't do this to you or to Mr. Carson. He's my savior and I owe him my life.

"You're not making any sense, Izzy."

"Just...just promise me you won't ruin his entire career, please. Please, Reina."

"Who—"

I'm cut off when she retrieves something from her apron and shoves it in my hand. "*Please*. If you care for me even a little, make my wish come true."

With that, she disappears down the hall. I attempt to chase her but Alex calls to me from up the stairs.

I stare at the small object Izzy has shoved into my hands: a flash drive.

What could all this be about? I guess it has to wait. After tucking the drive into my bag, I join Alex.

In his office, he tells me there's still no news about Reina. However, he's close to finding his contact.

That gives me so much hope, I can't help getting up and hugging Alex. He's not a warm person per se, but he's always treated me well on behalf of my dad.

My phone vibrates on my way out of Alex's office.

Asher: Come out.

The impatience of this man.

Reina: Why don't you come in?

Asher: The only place I'll be coming in tonight is your pussy.

My cheeks heat and I'm so glad I already left Alex's office.

Reina: Asshole.

Asher: Your ass too if you keep tempting me.

God, this man will be the death of me.

Before I step outside, I pull up Instagram and type a message to Cloud003. My chest is uneasy at the thought of doing this behind Asher's back, but he's left me no choice.

Jason and I need to talk one on one and solve whatever issues we have. I'm also sure he'll tell me about Arianna if Asher isn't around.

Reina-Ellis: Can we meet?

My fingers are stiff as I add the next word.

Reina-Ellis: Please?

I don't expect him to reply. It's a stretch, but I'm ready to try every option right now. Not only do I need to clear my name, I also need Asher to let go of the ghosts of the past.

My screen lights up.

Cloud003: Tomorrow. Seven. Blackwood Grand Hotel. Room 1003.

TWENTY-THREE

Reina

I stand in front of room 1003 at seven o'clock.

From what I've gathered about my odd relationship with Cloud003, we never met in person. We never had an encounter outside the Halloween parties.

So why does this hall seem familiar? Why does it feel like I've stood in a similar hallway before? I had the same feeling of the unknown.

No.

I have to do this. Besides, I'll just talk to him and go. I brought my security with me. If I don't come out in fifteen minutes, they'll call, and if I don't reply, they'll come for me.

I pull on the sleeves of my denim jacket. I dressed in jeans and a white top, nothing too out there.

Maybe all this tension is because I don't want to do any of this behind Asher's back.

I told him I was going out with Lucy and Naomi, and I

did catch a ride with them, but as soon as we were away from campus, I had my security guys drive me here.

They only report back to Alex, and he won't ask what I was doing here. Even if he does, he won't tell Asher.

Besides, I'm doing all this for that asshole. If he had let me talk to Jason last night, I wouldn't be forced to meet him in a hotel room as if I'm a cheater.

I'm *not* a cheater.

With one last deep breath, I knock on the door. A few seconds pass but no reply comes.

I knock again. Maybe he's not here yet? Well, it is seven, and he seems to be punctual, so—

My thoughts shatter when the door opens. The man standing in front of me isn't Jason.

No.

He's the last person I expected to find here.

Dark jeans accentuate his powerful thighs and a gray T-shirt stretches against his bulging muscles.

The eyes that shouldn't be staring at me right now capture my soul in their merciless hold.

"A-Asher?"

"The one and only, my slut." He grabs me by the arm and pulls me inside.

I'm too stunned to react or even move. It isn't until the door closes and he pushes me against it that I slowly come out of my stupor.

"W-what are you doing here?"

Oh, God. Oh, no.

My slut.

He called me his slut. Only one person calls me that, and it shouldn't be him. But maybe Asher saw our exchange? Maybe he knew I was meeting Jason and came to ruin it?

Why aren't any of those options registering in my head? Why does it keep rejecting them as if they hold no weight?

It's as if my head already knows the answer and those are not it.

"What are you doing here?" He drags his thumb down my cheek then grips my chin with both his fingers. "Weren't you supposed to have a night out with the *girls*?"

"I...I..."

"You lied. That's what you did. Do you know what happens when you lie to me?" He drags his nose down my cheek, and I hold my breath.

"Ash, I..." I clear my throat, as if that's enough to dissipate the cloud suffocating me. "I thought you were Jason."

"You thought I was Jason," he repeats, his voice gaining a lethal edge. "First you lied, then you thought I was Jason. Those are two strikes, my slut."

"D-don't call me that." Even as I say the words, I don't mean them. In a deep part of me, I like being called that by him just like before.

Just like before?

Oh, God. It is him.

It's really him.

"But you are..." He darts his tongue out and drags it over my bottom lip, making me shiver. "My *slut*."

I'm too lightheaded to think or form any words. I just stand there like a deer caught in the headlights. "B-but Lucy showed me a picture of you at a Halloween party in England last year. You...you couldn't have been here."

"That was a day before. I asked my friend to post it late."

"Why?"

"Because."

What is that supposed to mean? He didn't want me to find out? He was fucking with my head? Which exactly?

"I'm here." He licks my lips again, as if tasting them for the first time. "Why did you want to meet?"

When I don't speak, his fingers leave my jaw and wrap around my throat so tight, I nearly suffocate.

"What did you plan to do with Jason?"

"N-nothing," I choke out.

"You expect me to believe that?" He snarls at my face.

"I only wanted to ask him about Arianna. That's all."

"Why have you become such an expert liar?"

I glare up at him with all the energy I have considering his hand is cutting off my air supply. "I'm not lying. You *are*."

That causes him to loosen his grip a little, but he still has me pinned against the door. His free arm slams above my head so he's leaning on it and staring down at me. "I am?"

"You knew who I was all along, but you never once considered telling me who you are. You're a fucking liar, Ash."

It hits me then—all the things I told him via messages, every dark thought I talked about and confessed, not to mention all the sexual things we did in the past.

He owned a part of me and made me feel bad, thinking I cheated on him.

The asshole.

He strokes his thumb over my pulse point. "You knew."

"I...did?"

"You hid it well, but yes, you did. Last year, I was fucking you from behind while you were half-asleep and you called out my name." He sighs, the sound long and baffled. "You even asked me to stay. Why the fuck did you ask me to stay?"

It all comes back to me.

Not in flashbacks, but in little tangible memories. The way he held my hair as he fucked me with the urgency of a dying man, the way he kissed me hard and rough and made me come over and over again.

He was brutal, unapologetic, and used me up in every way possible. However, he pleased me, too. He looked at me with those bright green eyes through that black mask and told me without words how much he's obsessed with me, almost as much as I'm obsessed with him. He showed me in his actions how much being away never erased the connection we had.

Of course I knew who he was. I knew the moment I saw his eyes when he walked into the party. There are no pairs like them in the entire world—at least not for me.

There's no way the careful, standoffish Reina would've had a one-night stand. I was a calculating person who always looked ahead and plotted everything. One-night stands didn't fit my agenda.

The only reason I did it was because I knew it was Asher. The camouflage of the costumes gave me the anonymity I needed to surrender to him.

"Because I wanted you to," I say easily. "I wanted you to stay, Ash."

He pauses, his finger freezing at my throat. "You remember?"

"A few things," I murmur. "Those two times weren't the only ones, were they? There was another one before you went to England."

206 | RINA KENT

The memories are trickling in slowly, almost as if they're in the air and I have to jump up to catch them.

He speaks as if easing me into those recollections. "At Sebastian's lake house. It was dark and we were both drunk. I knew it was you because I was trailing your ass, but you didn't. At least, I thought you didn't." His nostrils flare. "You knew about that, too?"

"Of course I did." I smile a little. "I was trailing your ass, too. I just wasn't so obvious about it. That's what I did, you know. I watched from afar, stalked from afar, and told myself it was enough. That night, it wasn't. Could've been the alcohol or the fact that you were leaving the following morning and I would never see you again, but I had to be with you, even for one night."

Tears stream down my cheeks as the intensity of my emotions at the time slams into me. Even though I was drunk, nothing could've lessened the ache or the fact that I'd have to live in a world without him.

It was when the gloomy cloud struck the hardest.

"So I snuck to Bastian's lake house, knowing you'd follow me. I even removed the jacket and shoes on purpose. I needed to feel you, even if just once."

"Fuck, Reina." He slams his hand beside my head. "Fuck! Why didn't you say anything?"

"It would've broken the spell. You hated me back then, Ash." I gulp. "More than any time, I mean."

"So you made me believe you were fine with a one-night stand with a nobody after you always pushed me away?" He almost sounds bitter.

"You weren't a nobody. You were you."

"I thought you allowed a stranger to fuck you, Reina. I fucking hated you for it even though it was me."

"Small price to pay, I guess. Besides, I wouldn't have given my virginity to a stranger."

He pauses, and I pause, too, realizing what I just admitted.

Asher took my virginity. Fucking hell.

"I didn't know that." His brows furrow. "You didn't bleed or anything. You weren't in pain either."

I shrug, my cheeks heating. "Because it didn't hurt."

At that point, I'd wanted Asher for so long, having sex with him had become my favorite fantasy, so when it actually came true, I couldn't keep up with the fact that it was better than any fantasy I could've had.

Of course it didn't hurt; I was too aroused for that.

He picks me up in his arms and cuts the distance from the hotel's living room to the bedroom. I squeal as he throws me on the bed in pure caveman fashion. My heart stammers loud and hard as I lie on my back. Asher yanks down my jeans, and I grip his arm. "W-wait."

"I've waited long enough. I'm not waiting anymore."

"Let me call my security—they'll come up if I don't."

He groans in disapproval but throws me my bag. "You brought them for Jason?"

"As I said, I wasn't interested in anything but talking with him."

Which clearly isn't the case with Asher.

It takes me a second too long to retrieve my phone with my trembling fingers and dial the head of my security, Gaige.

"Miss Reina."

Asher doesn't break eye contact as he pulls his T-shirt over his head, revealing his sculpted abs. The tattoo ripples over his bicep as he reaches down to his pants and undoes the button, agonizingly slowly. Then he pushes his jeans and boxer briefs down his legs in one go.

Oh, God.

He's hard, thick, and ready. My own thighs clench in anticipation.

"Miss Reina?" Gaige's gravelly voice pulls me out of the strip show.

"Uh, yes. I'm good, Gaige. I'm spending the night with Asher. You can go back."

"We'll stay here, too."

"It's okay." I try not to sound breathy. "Nothing can happen to me here."

And I mean it. I feel safer than ever when I'm with this infuriating but deeply wounded man.

I'm wounded, too, have been since childhood, and being with him has given me the hope I'll be able to heal.

We'll be able to heal each other.

"Very well, Miss Reina. I'll stay just in case. Call me if anything happens."

Asher is stalking toward me and I couldn't focus on anything even if I tried. "Uh...yeah. Good night, Gaige."

I tap the hang-up button and push the phone and bag away.

"So you were a virgin, huh?" He crawls toward me, his hard thighs on either side of me.

He drags my jeans and panties down my legs in one ruthless go, and I fumble with my jacket and camisole. The straps get stuck in my hair and I nearly rip the strands out. It's Asher who untangles it and unclasps my bra, letting it fall to the pile of clothes on the floor.

With a push, I end up propped up on my elbows as his

body hovers over mine. The position is so intimate and…right. This is how Asher and I were always supposed to be.

"Answer me," he grunts near my mouth, hovering but not kissing.

The tease.

"I was." My breathing catches as I confess. "And you are the only one, Ash."

"The only one?"

"Yes. No one before you or after you. I know it for a fact."

Both his palms cage my face as he lowers his forehead to mine. "I thought I was the only one so hopeless for you."

"I was hopeless for you, too, Ash." I inhale his sandalwood and citrus scent, taking in his murmured confessions.

All of him.

The fact that he's Cloud003, the one who knows all my secrets and still wants me anyway, the fact that he wanted to hate me but he couldn't help coming back every year to be with me.

I inhale it all.

"You were my first and only, too, Reina."

My lips part, my heart flipping and thumping. "But you were in England and…oh, my God. Wait. You were a *virgin*?"

"At eighteen. How fucking pathetic is that?" He smiles but there's no humor behind it. "I guess I'm lucky you were too drunk to notice."

"Ash…"

"You were the only girl I wanted to kiss since I learned what kissing is and the only one I wanted to fuck since I learned what fucking means. All the others were nothing compared to you. I couldn't even get hard at the sight of them, and that didn't change when I went to England. Every time I felt the urge, I pulled out your picture or thought of the nights we had together and jerked off to them. I might have wanted to ruin you, but I could never stop the need to own you, too."

Asher's forehead remains connected to mine. With every word out of his mouth, my breathing turns deeper and shallower, harder and faster.

We weren't even in an actual relationship and he hated me, but he still remained faithful to me.

He didn't consider the other girls because he couldn't stop thinking about me.

"I never wanted any other man but you, and I never will." I wrap my arms around his neck. "You ruined me for everyone else."

His grunt is like music to my ears as he positions himself between my legs. "That's my slut."

Arousal coats my thighs at the rumble of his voice.

"Say it." His fingers wrap around my throat, the movement erotic and so utterly dominant.

"I'm…I'm…"

"That's not the word."

"I'm your…slut." Holy shit, why does it feel like such a turn-on to say it aloud?

"And you're mine."

"I'm yours."

The words catch in my throat as he thrusts balls-deep inside me. My entire body bucks off the bed, but his merciless hold on my neck keeps me prisoned in place. I wrap a hand around the arm holding me as my other one remains around his neck.

"You always let me fuck you dirty and hard." He grunts, picking up his pace. "I claimed both your pussy and your ass over and over again."

Oh God, that's why it didn't hurt the other time, and was even pleasing. It wasn't the first time or even the second.

"I own you, prom queen. All of you."

"Yes…" I choke on my breaths, my heart rate intensifying with the rhythm of his thrusts.

He does fuck me like I'm his slut. He flips me around and pounds into me from behind with my ass hanging off the edge then slaps my thighs and my ass cheeks until I scream his name.

He's not done.

As I shake and whimper with the force of my release, he maneuvers me so he's sitting on the bed and I'm settled on his lap with his hard cock still throbbing inside me. He takes me slower and unhurried as our chests beat in sync. He pulls out as much as he can before stabbing inside me again.

With every in and out, my body ignites and stars burst behind my lids. I wrap my arms around his neck as both his stronger arms wind around my back, stopping me from toppling to the ground.

We hug each other as he moves slowly inside me. I realize with tears in my eyes that I'm not his slut now; I'm almost his…queen.

His one and only.

That thought alone pushes me to the pleasurable heights of another crippling orgasm. I scream his name, my teeth finding his shoulder and my nails digging into his skin. His lips find the hollow of my neck as he grunts and spills inside me.

My eyes flutter closed, exhaustion rearing on my nerve endings. He always fucks me so thoroughly I only have the energy to sleep afterward.

This is all I ever wanted.

All I ever needed in life, to sleep in his arms and feel so utterly safe.

"Why Cloud003, though?" I murmur in my sleepy haze.

"Cloud because of Gray, my middle name. 003 because of the day I first met you, January 3rd. It's the reason behind this room number, too—1003."

I smile against his skin. Damn this man and the lengths he went to for this.

I love you, my mind screams. *I love you so much, and it kills me to think you don't feel the same.*

TWENTY-FOUR

Reina

The sound of vibrating pulls me from a deep sleep. I groan as I flip on my side and try to fumble about, but a strong arm keeps me pinned in place.

A smile breaks across my lips as I slowly crack my eyes open. Asher's unearthly face is a few inches away from mine, in a deep sleep. He probably hasn't slept well since two days ago, and his thick brows are furrowed together.

I place a finger in the middle and try to alleviate the crease.

Isn't it unfair for someone to be so handsome even when he sleeps?

The phone continues vibrating.

The clock on the wall reads eleven in the evening; we were so exhausted we fell into a deep slumber.

Asher's face becomes peaceful again as soon as I relieve the furrow. I slowly lift his arm from my midsection and slip from the crook of his body.

The phone stops vibrating and I think about going back to sleep until I see the missed call.

Izzy.

She wouldn't call me this late without a reason. Did something happen to Alex?

I run to the bathroom, put on a robe, and then go back in the room, grab my bag and phone, and duck to the other half of the room.

As soon as I'm out of Asher's earshot, I call Izzy back. She answers after the first ring.

"What is it, Izzy?" I pant. "Is everyone okay?"

"I...uh...I'm sorry for calling this late. No one is hurt, don't worry."

Thank God. I flop on the couch, releasing a breath. "What is it then? Do you need anything?"

"I was wondering if you watched the video."

"The video?"

"The one on the flash drive."

Right. She gave me that yesterday. I got distracted by hiding my meeting with Cloud003 from Asher, so I forgot about it.

"Not yet."

"You should," she whispers. "Please watch it. And Reina?"

"Yes?"

"I'm so sorry."

The line goes dead. I stare at the black screen for a second too long. Izzy has been acting strange since yesterday. Maybe if I watch this footage, I'll figure out why.

I search inside my bag until I find the small black flash drive. I plug it into the hotel's TV and keep the volume low as I open the video file.

The quality appears odd, the angle covert, almost like that video Jason showed me the other time.

Only now, the angle captures Arianna from the front. She's looking up, probably at the person filming this.

Sitting on one of the cushions in the pool house, she twirls a bra on her finger and laughs. "Can you believe how that little bitch fell for a bra in Gray's bag? She thinks she's so smart, but she's too easily manipulated."

"Asher, too." Jason—it's his voice.

"Unfortunately, yeah," she says with mock sarcasm. "All I had to do was threaten Stanford with exposing his pedophile picture collection and he called Reina's name like a parrot when I was sucking him off."

"Did it feel good?" Jason asks in a slightly thick voice.

"Good?" She laughs. "Nothing feels good to me, Jace. Everything is like a rehearsed play. It felt like sucking plastic. But since I knew the right buttons to push, I made him feel good. Besides, Gray believed it. Win-win."

"You're bad." There's a smile in Jason's voice.

"Thank you." She feigns a curtsy. "It's getting boring playing with them, you know. Gray and Reina were these two people who looked at each other like they found salvation. It was interesting to watch them dissolve, to hold on to that something even though they keep hurting. I had to know what that infuriating connection was that I couldn't understand. It helped that they cared for me. It made messing with their lives easier. A rumor here, some chaos there, and they just keep cracking. It's *fascinating*. Gray even believed Reina was behind all those dares, and Reina thought it was Gray's revenge against her so she kept her mouth shut when everyone accused her."

A deep laugh comes from Jason. "Only you would ruin the two people who love you the most, Ari."

"Love." She cocks her head to the side like a maniac. "What is that? And why should I care about it? The only reason I keep Gray and Reina close is because it's fun to toy with them. The king and queen of school are under the most insignificant student's thumb. Hashtag fall of a kingdom."

"Come on, you never cared about them?"

"No. They're just there to serve a purpose I need and then they're out. Mom used to teach me how to be caring and attentive and it was fucking annoying. I'm glad that bitch died and left me in peace. At least Dad doesn't care for shit and Gray became easier to fool as we grew up."

"And now what?" Jason asks. "You said something about Reina finding out?"

"Hmm, yeah." She taps her mouth. "I think she figured something out after I confessed I love Gray today. He didn't suspect anything when I confessed I loved Reina, but the bitch is smarter than I give her credit for. She ruined my plan, and I'll make her pay."

"How?"

She sighs. "It's getting boring anyway so I might as well go for the grand finale."

"What grand finale?" Jason asks.

"Breaking them up once and for all. And Jace?"

"Yeah?"

"Continue my legacy. I know you yearn for chaos deep inside, so once I make the fire, don't let it burn out."

"You mean keep Asher and Reina apart?"

"Yeah. After I'm done with them, they'll never come together again anyway, but just in case, don't allow them to reunite."

"Why don't you make sure of it yourself, Ari?"

She stares at the camera as if she knew it was there all along. My palms turn clammy at the vacant, empty look in her eyes.

That's not a person; that's a monster.

"This world is too small for me."

The screen goes black, but I keep staring at it. A tear slides down my cheek, then another follows and another. I can't stop them even if I wanted to.

I loved Arianna. I thought of her as some sort of replacement for Reina, but she never once cared for me. All she was interested in was proving herself by manipulating mine and Asher's love for her.

And Jason...

Shit.

He's been in on it since the beginning. He shared Ari's brand of crazy and made me think Asher was my worst enemy, and while he was in some ways, it wasn't his fault. He didn't do it because he truly hated me; he did it because he was compelled to.

I would've done the same if I were in his shoes.

It's such an ugly position to be in.

I reach for the remote to turn off the TV then a large presence appears in my peripheral vision. I gasp, the remote falling from my fingers and clattering to the ground.

Asher stands at the entrance of the bedroom, only wearing boxer briefs. He's still staring at the blank screen like I was a few seconds ago.

From his blank expression, it seems he watched it—or at least most of it. He continues focusing on the TV as if Arianna is still there, saying she never cared for us, saying her brother who sacrificed his youth for her happiness and matured early to become her parent and her support was easy to fool, saying all she cared about was destroying him.

God, he's not reacting—not at all.

It's even scarier than if he trashed the place.

Even his hands fall on either side of him like lifeless body parts. There's no clenching of his fists or ticking of his jaw.

He's gone numb.

No, I won't let her take him away from me. Not again.

Arianna won't peek her head out from the grave to ruin our lives once more. She succeeded in the past, but that won't be happening again.

I stagger on unsteady feet and tiptoe toward him as if afraid he'll snap any second. He doesn't move, not even when I stand in front of him, my toes almost touching his.

"Ash…" I coax.

No answer.

I take his hand in mine. It's heavy and unmoving and… cold. So damn cold.

"Ash, look at me."

His gaze strays from the TV to mine. There's so much pain in there, so many years lost on hate, revenge, violence.

So much missed time.

"It wasn't your fault." My voice is emotional despite my attempt to speak in a neutral tone. "It wasn't *our* fault. We just loved her too much to notice it."

He says nothing, but his jaw tightens so hard I'm scared something will happen to him.

What if I lose him?

What if she succeeded and this is the end?

What if—

"I'm so sorry." His voice is barely above a murmur.

My brows furrow. "What?"

His arms wrap around me in a tight hug that nearly cuts off my breath. "I'm so fucking sorry, Reina."

If possible, his hug tightens more around me. It says so much more than his words are telling me. It says how much he regrets the past, how much he wished to never let me go.

So I hug him back because I have those same regrets.

We lost so much time. We floundered and drowned and couldn't come up for air for so long.

All that pain fades away now, almost as if it were never there.

I let him carry me back to bed. We don't speak after that.

We just watch each other, limbs wrapped around one another as we fall asleep.

We're both wounded and need to recuperate.

A nightmare startles me awake. There were harsh blue-green eyes laughing at me, mocking me, telling me I could never escape my fate.

A tear slides down my cheek as I open my lids. A thumb wipes the tear away.

Those dark green eyes collide with mine as he slowly wipes the tear. His hand doesn't leave my face even after all the tears are gone. His strong hand cradles my cheek as he watches me intently as if I'll turn into smoke and mirrors.

It's late, like two or three in the morning late, but it seems like he slept too little, if he slept at all.

Seeing him in so much pain and not being able to talk

about it kills me slowly. Asher has always been the silent type who directed his pain inside instead of purging it, and that killed him, slowly but surely.

I can't have him keep all of it in, not after what all we've both been through.

"Trouble sleeping," I murmur as if a louder voice will lift the cloak surrounding us.

"I can't get her voice or face out of my head." His words are low and filled with so much pain, they gut me. "I can't believe that's my baby sister, the same Ari I sacrificed so much for. I should've seen the signs, or stopped and questioned when I saw those fucking signs."

"Hey." I snake my palm up his naked chest and rest it against his calm heartbeat, his almost dead pulse. "We couldn't have known, she was too strategic about it, and we were too young and with too many communication issues."

"Communication issues she fed on and used against us."

"Unfortunately."

"Unfortunately?" His voice rises a little. "I think this calls for a stronger word than that. Our lives were broken to fucking pieces."

"Not all our lives," I say hopefully, almost pathetically.

"Not all our lives."

My heart thunders so loud, it takes me a moment to gather my wits around me and ask to be sure. "Just the past?"

"Just the past."

"I missed you so much, Ash," I confess and another tear slides down my cheek. "Those three years were hell, absolute emptiness. I hated you so much for leaving me behind, for never looking back or trying to get me to you. Arianna might have killed us but you killed me by abandoning me. You were the only thread I had in life after Dad's death and you just cut me off so brutally."

"I'm sorry." He wipes my tear with the pad of his thumb. "If it's of any comfort, I killed myself, too. There hasn't been a moment I haven't thought about you."

I can't stop the tears even if I want to. The more he wipes them away, the harder they fall.

"Reina…" he murmurs my name like a prayer he's been dying to say.

"I don't want to fight. Not tonight." I wrap my arms around his midsection and bury my face in his chest.

His strong hand covers the small of my back as he buries his nose in my hair, inhaling me in. "I don't want to fight either. Not tonight, not ever."

We wake up to the sound of harsh pounding on the door. I groan as I make out Asher's shadow leaving the room and going to answer it.

"What the fuck are you doing here?" His grave voice pulls me from my sleep-induced haze.

I jump out of bed, wrapping the robe tight around me.

"Get out of here." Asher's voice turns lethal.

I peek out and pause. Detective Daniels stands in the middle of the living area wearing a smug grin and flashing a piece of paper at Asher.

"Not today, Carson. I have an arrest warrant for Miss Reina Ellis."

TWENTY-FIVE

Reina

I only come out after changing back into my clothes and doing my makeup. Now, I understand why Old Reina needed to do that whenever she went out. I didn't like being put under the spotlight if I didn't have some sort of shield. My perfect face and appearance were it.

It was a defense mechanism to hide my true feelings. I was a pro at that.

Detective Daniels waits for me with two buff officers wearing hats near the door. He's had a smug grin on his face since he revealed the arrest warrant.

Perspiration coats my skin as one bleak thought after another barges into my mind. What if they actually found Reina's body?

No. Alex said his guy sent him a text after that night saying she was safe.

My sister is a fighter; she wouldn't just die.

Asher paces the length of the room, a phone to his ear. "Pick the fuck up, Alexander."

"It's okay." I place a hand on his arm, forcing him to stop. "Go find him at the firm. He's probably in a meeting."

Still clutching the phone, he palms both my cheeks and tugs up so I'm staring straight at his pained eyes. "I'll get you out of there. I promise."

My limbs start to shake as if about to give up on me. If he keeps touching me, I'll surrender to all those gloomy thoughts and break.

I can't do that when I have to find my sister.

I try to wiggle away from his touch but he pins me in place, the forest green color of his eyes turning somber. "Are you running away from me, prom queen?"

"No." *Yes.*

"You can't leave me, not anymore." His lips brush against mine in a brief, heartbreaking kiss. "You're my world now."

Tears well in my eyes, and I wrench myself from him before I start crying.

I can't do that. Not now.

I stride toward the detective and the officers. My heart begs for one last glance at Asher, but I deny that request. I need to be strong for this, and I can't do that if I keep thinking about Asher's last words.

As soon as I'm in front of them, Detective Daniels tells me I'm under arrest for murder and reads me my rights, then he leans in to whisper, "I told you I'd get you."

My expression doesn't change, but my pulse rises at the contempt in his tone.

I walk with them down the hall and through the lobby where people stare at me all the way. Gaige runs toward me with a frown etched between his brows, but I stop him. "It's okay, just try to reach Alex."

He gives a sharp nod and retrieves his phone. My only option is to remain silent until Alex shows up. I'm sure he'll be able to shut the detective down like before, that is if they didn't really find a body.

The officers don't say a word. They're bulky with tattoos sneaking down their sleeves. One has an untamed beard and the other has a permanent sneer. Is that a scar over his jaw?

One of the officers takes the wheel as the other one opens the back door. Daniels retrieves cuffs and tries to restrain me.

I pull my hands free. "I didn't resist arrest—there's no need for those."

"I'm the one who decides whether you resisted or not," he snarls then snaps the handcuffs on my wrists.

I gulp at the feeling of being handled like a criminal. I hate this. The detective shoves me inside so I'm sandwiched between him and the other officer.

The pungent smell of coffee and smoke fill the car and the windows are securely closed. Of course. I try to breathe through my mouth as we drive down Blackwood's streets.

We go for about fifteen minutes in suffocating silence. They don't talk and I'm determined to keep my right to remain silent.

Why is the station so far away?

Something vibrates at my side before the officer beside me picks up. He speaks in Russian, and even though mine is rusty, I recognize the words loud and clear.

We got her.

Oh, God. Oh, no.

I try to keep my expression neutral, to not show I know what he's saying.

This must be Ivan Sokolov, my mom's killer, the reason Reina disappeared.

Now, he's coming after me.

I stare out the window and sure enough, we're out of the civilized area and headed to the highway that leads to the forest.

Shit, shit.

Think. I need to think about a way out of this. What would Mom have done under the circumstances?

"I need to use the bathroom," I say in a bored voice.

"You'll do that when we get to the station," Detective Daniels says.

He's in on this, too. He must be. That's why he was so focused on my case like a parasite. It wasn't for justice; it was because he works for Ivan.

"Well, it's urgent. You got me out in a rush." I roll my eyes. "I'm fine if you want piss all over your seat."

The officer beside me curses me in Russian.

Well, fuck you, too.

He taps the barrier separating us from the driver and tells him something. They exchange tense words for a bit and I keep a bored façade as I try to figure out what they're saying.

One of them is saying no, and the other says the boss won't be happy if something happens to me. Finally, they decide to make a stop at a gas station. Detective Daniels is the one to accompany me.

"Behave." He flashes me his gun as he stands at the entrance.

I go inside and resist the urge to melt to the ground and have a freak-out party.

Holy shit. They're taking me to the Russian mafia.

My phone and bag are in the hotel room so I have nothing on me right now.

Pacing the length of the restroom, I stop near the mirror. There's a chipped part that's nearly falling off.

I don't hesitate to grab it and hide it in the pocket of my denim jacket as I turn on the faucet.

My only option is to get rid of Daniels. The others are in the car, so I have maybe five minutes before they come looking.

You're Mia's Sokolov's daughter and Nikolai Sokolov's granddaughter. You can do this.

A loud bang comes from the outside. "Are you done?"

I stare at myself one last time in the mirror.

You're a survivor, just like your mother, just like Reina.

The knob turns at the same time I open the door.

"Finally," he grunts. "Walk in front."

This is the only chance I have. My fingers tremble over the edge of the shard, cutting the skin.

Now or never.

I pretend to walk in front of Daniels then I turn abruptly and jam the shard of glass into his neck, just above the collarbone. His eyes widen and it takes him a second to realize what happened.

As he falls back, I fumble in his pocket and snatch away the plastic bag that has my bracelet then tuck it safely in my pocket.

This is mine, and he had no right to take it.

He reaches a hand for me, but I'm already gone.

I don't focus on him or the thud I hear as he hits the ground. I don't focus on the oozing blood, surrounding him in a pool as he wheezes.

The only thing I focus on is my escape route.

I dart past him toward the gas station's shop. I'll use their phone and call for help. Then I'll keep running or hide away until the guys in the car are gone.

I'm in front of the store when a strong blow lands on the back of my neck. My feet fail me and I fall to my knees and then to my side, my vision turning blurry.

Russian voices hover over me, far then near then almost as if they're speaking from a well. Someone kicks me in the ribs. I want to scream but no voice comes out.

Instead, darkness swallows me whole.

I'm so sorry, Mama.

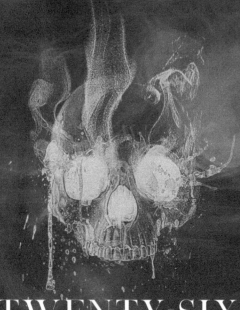

TWENTY-SIX

Asher

I barge into Alexander's office, my temper about to boil over. The secretary runs after me, telling me he has a meeting and all that blah blah blah, but I'm not hearing her.

The way here was a fucking blur. I drove like a madman and thankfully didn't get myself or anyone else killed.

I can't erase the way Reina looked as she went with them. That vulnerability she hides so well was visible in the slight tremors in her hands and how she tried to leave me as fast as she could.

But she'll never leave.

Now that I know what Ari did, I'll never let Reina out of my sight. Even before knowing Ari's plans, I was already figuring out a way to keep Reina.

I meant it—I can't stay away.

Ari, my baby sister Ari…she was more messed up than I

could've predicted, and it hurt like a motherfucker to hear her say those words.

On the flip side, it gave me some closure.

There'll always be pain whenever I think of my only sibling, the one I lived for at one point. There'll be days where I'll stop and ask myself if I could've done better, understood her better, but that day won't be now.

Alexander pauses mid-speech as I stride to the center of the conference room. When he figures out I'm here to stay, he addresses his audience. "That'll be all for today. Email me the first draft."

Just like that, the hotshot lawyers who were sitting around the table scatter.

The secretary apologizes, telling him she couldn't stop me, but he dismisses her too. As the door hisses closed behind her, he leans over. "To what do I owe this visit?"

"Reina has been arrested by that fucking detective."

"What?" He straightens, nonchalant mood disappearing.

"He had an arrest warrant."

"He can't have an arrest warrant—there was no body."

"Well, do something." My temper flares, nearly getting the better of me.

"I won't have you order me around, Asher."

I charge toward him until I'm standing toe to toe with him. We're the same height, but I'm wider than him. The only reason I'm not punching him is because Reina needs his skills. "You were never a father to Ari and me, but you were always someone she could lean on. Don't fail her, too."

"I don't need you to tell me that." He retrieves his phone from his pocket and dials a number. After a few seconds, he says, "Alexander Carson speaking. My client Reina Ellis has been arrested by Detective Daniels, and I would like to know the details."

He listens for a few seconds then his brows furrow.

Fuck. That's not a good sign.

"Where is the detective?"

After listening, he hangs up with a curse.

"What is it?" I ask even though I don't want to hear the answer.

"They're not at the station."

"But it's been more than half an hour since they left."

"They don't know the detective's whereabouts." He slams his fist on the table. It's the first time I've seen him this agitated.

"What do you mean they don't know his whereabouts? There were officers and…" I trail off. "Do you think—"

My words are cut off when his phone rings. He puts a hand up. "This is my guy."

I remain silent as he speaks.

"Alexander Carson…yes…what do you mean she's with them? … How about Rai? Where is she?" He remains motionless then lets the hand holding the phone fall to his side. "Fucking hell."

The tendons in my neck bulge. "What now?"

"The Russian Mafia has her. She's with Ivan Sokolov."

My head spins and my worst nightmares start to materialize in front of me.

Reina hurt.

Reina tortured.

Reina—

I shake my head. I won't let that happen, not now after all the distance we crossed. Besides, I promised to find her.

I fucking *promised*.

"What are we going to do now?" My voice is calm considering the disorder in my brain.

"My guy said he and Rai are out of this situation. It's too risky."

"We can't just do nothing."

He releases a breath. "I'm thinking."

I pace the length of the room, my head filling with the scenarios Reina could find herself in.

Each one is more terrible than the previous.

She might have lived on the run in the past, but that was a long time ago. She knows nothing about mafia life now.

Reina is as clueless as your next normal citizen.

My phone vibrates and I retrieve it, about to silence it. The unknown number makes me stop in my tracks.

I answer, "Who is this?"

The voice on the other end is the last one I expected to hear. "Hello, Asher."

TWENTY-SEVEN

Reina

A slap across the face startles me awake.

For a second, I'm too disoriented to realize where I am. It's dark, strange, and smells of humidity.

Then everything crashes down on me in one go.

Daniels, the officers who spoke in Russian, and then—

My head jerks up and I freeze.

Light blue eyes stare down at me with malice so tangible I feel it crawling along my skin. He's wearing a black suit, and his whitish blond hair is cut short, showcasing his square jawline.

I know who he is even before he says a word.

My mom's nightmare.

The one who killed her then took my sister.

The one who killed my dad.

The one who made my childhood hell and orphaned me.

Ivan Sokolov.

I wiggle in my seat, but the tightly secured ropes keep me

in place. I'm sitting on a metal chair in the middle of a sterile room. The earlier smell of humidity is replaced by something more potent: blood. No—piss and blood.

A shudder goes through me at the thought of what they do here.

The lamp hanging from the ceiling barely gives me a sense of time or space. I have no idea how long I've been out or if we're even still on American soil. Maybe we're in Russia already? It's a terrible thought, but I need to weigh all the possibilities. This is someone who slaughtered my entire family and wouldn't hesitate to end my life.

I stare at him with all the hatred I've felt for years, the grudge, the need for revenge.

"If it isn't the other *suka*." His voice is slightly accented but otherwise refined. "You two are so much like Mia. Too bad she didn't live to see you grow up."

I bite my lower lip to not lash out. I recognize what he's doing, trying to bring out my anger so he can have me in the palm of his hand, but he should know looks aren't the only thing Reina and I got from Mom. We have her wit, too.

Realizing I won't fall for his bait, Ivan smiles, and it's too deranged, too...fucked up, almost like a sick *Game on* of sorts.

"Now, Reina, a birdie has told me you're regaining your memories, and I would like to know where your sister disappeared to."

"Well, your birdie is wrong."

I curse internally. It must've been Detective Daniels. That asshole was keeping an eye on me on Ivan's behalf all this time until he was sure I'd have information for this jerk.

He must've figured out I'm regaining my memories from our last encounter.

Ivan slaps me across the face so hard my body jerks with the sting. *That hurts.*

"Lose the fucking attitude. All of you spawn of Nikolai need lessons in manners."

I bite down the pain and stare at him. This is between me and him, and if he thinks I'll give up easily, he must not know how much of Mom's survival instinct lives within me.

"I'll be nice." He crouches in front of me, almost like a doting uncle. "Tell me where Rai is and I'll let you go."

An acute sense of relief washes over me at his words. If he's searching for her then he thinks she's alive, and if he can't find her, that should mean she's safe.

At least that's what my brain hopes for.

"You want me to believe you'll let me go?"

"You're right—I won't." He laughs; it's short and sharp. "I can't rule if any of Nikolai's filthy blood live on. If that fucker bodyguard hadn't taken Rai that day, both of you would be dead by now. I had to keep you alive to draw her out."

She's alive. Reina is alive. I can almost feel her breathing now.

"I'm a generous man, Reina. If you tell me where she is, I promise your end won't be painful—just a single bullet like Mia. If you don't, well…you'll just die from torture and I'll throw your head in front of Rai before she takes her last breaths." He stands to his full height, almost casting a shadow over me. "What will it be?"

My spine jerks and spasms of fear dance along it. I have no doubt he'll follow through on his threats. He must be under a lot of pressure from the other leaders, and he knows all too well he won't be able to rule without the ledger Reina has.

He's a desperate man, and desperate people have no limits, especially desperate, dangerous people.

What he doesn't realize is that I'm a desperate woman, too. Since I lost Mom nine years ago, I've been half-empty waiting for the day I can return the favor of Reina saving me, hoping against hope she survived and is alive somewhere.

That chance is today. Now, I'm desperate to save her, desperate to see that light in her eyes again.

To say I'm not scared of what Ivan can do to me would be a lie. Not only is he a member of the mafia, he's also successfully carried out numerous hits. My limbs are slightly shaking and I couldn't stop them even if I wanted to.

I might've had gloomy thoughts before, but I never once carried it out because deep down, I knew there was so much more I should be living for. There are people who love me even though I've been an imposter since I was twelve.

There was also someone, the boy who turned into a messed-up man, the boy I loved and the man I fell in love with all over again.

There are many reasons why I should hold on to life, but now that my sister's life is at stake, I'd rather die than turn my back on her again.

Besides, it's not a lie as I say, "I don't know."

He raises his hand and I brace myself for the slap, but he punches me in the face. I jerk in my seat as blood explodes on my lower lip and I taste metal. Coughing, I meet his gaze again.

It's filled with the hunger for power, the need to rise, to crush everyone. It's almost laughable how obvious he is. I don't laugh, of course, because I still need my life.

"My nice phase is coming to an end, Reina." He slams a

hand against my face, only allowing me to look at him through his fat, meaty fingers. "Where. Is. She?"

"I d-don't know." I choke on the words.

His next punch makes me see stars. My teeth chatter and my fingers tighten against each other behind my back. I cough up the blood that gathers in my mouth.

"Last chance." He closes in on me, his face mere inches from mine. "Where the fuck is she?"

People say you can never see your end coming. It happens too suddenly, and once you realize it, it's too late.

I see it, though—my end. I see it in his unfeeling blue eyes and the desperation they reek of. He'll kill me no matter what I do or say. He's been planning that since the moment he got his men to kidnap me.

I might not be able to finish him, but I have belief Reina would. I hope she makes him regret the day he was born. I know she'll get justice for Mom, Dad, and me.

"I don't know." My voice is broken due to how I speak over the blood. "Even if I did, I would never tell you." Then I do the only thing I can under the circumstances. I spit blood on his clean-shaven face, the droplets splattering on his skin. "You'll die like a fucking pig."

For a second, he watches me with wide eyes, as if he never expected me to do that. I smile with triumph, but it doesn't last as he punches me again.

This time, the chair topples and I fall backward. My limbs don't catch me since they're tied, and my head hits the ground. Pain explodes in my body as a boot connects with my ribs, knocking the air out of my lungs.

I gasp for air and find nothing.

A pop sounds in my body as he kicks me again and again.

"I'll make your death the most painful possible." He calls a name and the door opens. I barely hear the words or make out my surroundings.

It's blurry and dark, shadows dancing in my vision as if they're real.

"Bring me my tools," Ivan says with a smirk. "We have a long night ahead."

It's supposed to scare me, but I'm too numb for that, too... out of this world.

One face keeps flickering in my mind as my vision slowly withers away.

Asher...our last encounter and the way I ran away from him...

I wish I hadn't. I wish I'd kissed him harder and told him I love him.

I wish I'd let go of my shackles and confessed my feelings earlier. Maybe everything would be different.

Maybe I wouldn't be lying here, choking on my own blood and leaving the world with so many regrets.

But it's too late.

It's true, you know. The end comes once you realize it's too late.

Ivan's shoe slams into my ribs and darkness sucks me into its clutches.

TWENTY-EIGHT

Asher

Alexander didn't want me to come here, but fuck him and anyone who thinks I'd stay still when Reina's fate is unknown.

After I received that phone call, we shot into action.

The only one who matters right now is Reina.

I haven't been able to breathe since she went out of my sight this morning. It's as if I'm living on borrowed time and borrowed air until I find her.

And I'll find her even if it's the last thing I do.

"Check your vest," says the man at my side. His name is Kyle, as Alexander introduced us. No idea if that's a real name or an alias, but I don't give two fucks right now.

If he has the skills to get Reina out of that hellhole then he can be an alien for all I care.

"It's fine."

"That's what amateurs say." He has a slight Northern Irish

accent and appears to be in his late twenties to early thirties. No idea why he sounds familiar when we've never met before.

He's too laid back for all the hitman work Alexander said he does. According to my father, he's the best man for mafia-centered jobs, and I trust Alexander to always find the best for shady jobs.

Kyle clicks his gun and hides a few knives in his waistband and offers me one. It's only me and him and another hitman who runs in his crowd.

Naturally, Kyle and his sniper friend don't function well with the police, so they'll do the rescue and disappear before cops show up.

The sniper is positioned somewhere on the opposite building. Since I can't see him—and I'm looking—it should mean he's good.

"If you hinder me, I'll knock you out." Kyle doesn't look up from his weapons as he says the words.

"Give me a gun."

He pauses. "Do you even know how to use one?"

"Yes, I do. I've had shooting lessons." And boxing ones and a whole lot of fucked-up shit I thought would keep me from acting out my obsession with Reina.

They didn't.

"Lessons and real life are different." He points the gun to my chest and clicks the magazine. "There would be a hole here and a lot of blood. Just saying, in case you're squeamish."

"I tortured a man nearly to death for her. If you think I would have second thoughts about shooting any motherfucker who hurts her, you don't know who you're dealing with."

The fact that he's holding a gun straight against my chest

doesn't faze me or scare me. Determination shoots through my veins, and all I can think about is finding her.

Kyle drops the gun in my hand. "Count your bullets and never leave yourself without backup."

I give a curt nod as we slip into the back entrance of what looks like an old factory. Like some apocalypse, the area is deserted and there are no people in sight. It's the perfect location to dispose of a body.

Those thoughts won't consume me.

Reina will be fine. She's a survivor.

As Kyle instructed, I remain behind him. He's wearing a white T-shirt and black slacks as if he just left a business meeting. His build is tall and fit, and he makes no sound.

I try to walk as quietly as possible, but I don't match the way he moves through the shadows as if he belongs in them.

The inside of the factory is shabbier than the outside. The windows are half-broken, allowing the wind to slide into the space. I stare at the roof, speculating if the sniper has a good range from here.

"Forget about him," Kyle says in his bored voice. "Imagine you're on your own. If you keep waiting for others to save you, you'll die."

That's true in some ways.

"Why did you agree to do this?" I ask. He sure as hell didn't seem on board when he talked to Alexander.

"It's what I'm paid to do."

Suddenly, he stops at the corner and places a finger to his mouth before grabbing his gun with both hands. He motions at me to remain where I am. I do, tightening my hold around my own pistol.

This means we have company. I peek around the corner

and sure enough, Detective Daniels and the two officers who took Reina stand in front of a metal door.

They're laughing and drinking as if this is some sort of a celebration.

Blood pumps in my veins with the need to murder them. I knew Daniels was shady. I should've suspected he was working with these motherfuckers.

I expect Kyle to sneak up or to stay here until the danger passes, but he retrieves a suppressor, hooks it to the tip of his gun, and goes out. Just like that, he's out.

His eyes remain the same, bored and motionless as he clicks a few times. Curses and a commotion erupt in Russian from where he's aiming, but the sound of his muffled gunshots are louder.

Then all sounds disappear as he motions at me to follow him.

In front of the door lie three men with three clean shots to their foreheads. Daniels' neck is covered with a bandage, but that the least of his problems. He and the other men have their mouths wide open, and their eyes stare at nothing.

Impressive.

No wonder Alexander thinks highly of Kyle when he rarely does that with anyone.

I should probably feel something about seeing three people murdered, but I don't. They took Reina from me and they deserve a fate worse than death.

Kyle kicks the bodies away to walk to the door. "Ivan should be in there, and he's a good shooter. Stay here."

"No. Reina is in there, too."

He faces me, his gun lying by his side. "If you die, I'll tell your dad you went in for suicide."

"Fine with me."

A smirk curves his lips. "Deal."

"No deal." The voice comes from behind us, and both of us spin around.

Reina.

She's wearing jeans and a black hoodie that camouflages half her face, but I know it's her—or rather, the original Reina, not *my* Reina.

They're so similar, I thought Reina was the one who called me earlier today. They look so much alike, too—face, body type, everything.

Except, I realize it's not my Reina. She's not the girl who had me whipped then destroyed me then slowly put me back together again.

Kyle tilts his head. "What are you doing here?"

"Ending this."

"We decided we'd do this my way, Rai."

"You decided. I never agreed to that." She squirms free from his hold. "If you go in there, raising your gun, Ivan won't hesitate to shoot her."

"Well, genius." He speaks with mockery. "If you go in there, he won't hesitate to shoot you, too."

"He will."

The calmness and determination in her voice and face are so similar to Reina's when she's set on doing something. There's no changing her mind.

"I have something he wants," Rai says.

"Your only lifeline."

"No." She smiles. "His."

She brushes past him and to the door. Kyle attempts to grab her again, but she pushes away from him, holds a phone to her ear, and speaks something in Russian. It sounds smooth and authoritative, like someone who knows exactly what they're doing and why they're doing it.

Since she called when I was in Alexander's office, I knew Rai had a plan bigger than sending Kyle and his assassin after Ivan.

"For fuck's sake," Kyle says after she hangs up, but he doesn't try to stop her again.

She smiles at me; it's slight and barely there. "Let's get my sister back."

With purposeful strides, she pounds on the metal door and doesn't even blink at the corpses lying in front of it. "I'm here, Ivan. I have the ledger."

Kyle creeps to her right and I stand to her left as we wait for a response.

One second passes, two—

The door opens with a creak. A blond man stands in the entrance, filling it up and disallowing any view of the inside.

"Rai…" he says in an accented voice, grinning. "Isn't this a surprise? You even brought the traitor."

Kyle lifts a shoulder. "I was never with you."

Now I know why he sounded familiar. Although he feigned a Russian accent at the time, this is the man who was at the forest the night Reina—and supposedly Rai—were assaulted. He pretended to be with them but was actually saving Rai. That's why she's been relatively safe since.

"If you want the ledger, you can have it." Rai steps forward.

"Where is it?" The humor Ivan tried to fake disappears.

"Where's my sister?"

A red drop hits the ground and I follow the line, realizing

the source is his hands, which he's been hiding since he opened the door.

Reina…?

"See, it's a bit too late. She wouldn't talk, and you know I hate the silent ones." He pauses. "She's not dead yet, though, so give me the ledger and I might let her breathe another second."

The need to pull the trigger and shoot him in the head overwhelms me, but I can't do that, not without knowing how many of his men are in there. What if I hurt him and the others kill Reina?

"My sister first." Rai's voice doesn't change.

He extends a hand. "The ledger, Rai. Don't make this too difficult and try to take what was never yours."

"That's you, not me. But fine, I guess you win."

"I always win, *suka*. Now give it."

Rai reaches a hand under her hoodie and Ivan's eyes light up like a kid.

Instead of a ledger, she pulls out something glinting and grabs him by the hand, going straight to his eyes with a knife. His roar of pain can be heard in the long empty hallway.

He reaches blindly at her. The knife in his right eye gushes blood all over his cheek and neck and down to his shirt.

I push him aside in his stupor and run inside. If there is anyone in there and they've hurt—

The sight in front of me stops me in my tracks. Reina lies on the ground, tied to a chair. Her blond strands are smudged with red. Everything is red—her face, her arms, and even her clothes.

Fuck!

I run toward her, tuning out the commotion between Rai, Kyle, and Ivan. Crouching in front of Reina, I push the strands over her cheeks and find one of her eyes swollen, the other closed shut. Her lips are bloodied and busted. If I hadn't recognized her as my Reina from afar, I wouldn't have known it's truly her.

I cut through the wires around her wrist like a maniac with the knife Kyle gave me. I hold her hand mine and wait with a held breath to see the rise and fall of her chest, the proof she's alive and won't put me through the torture of living without her anymore.

A small sound rips from her, something that resembles a whimper or a moan of pain—or both.

I release a breath and stand up.

The fucker tortured her. He beat her up until he erased her features and turned her unrecognizable.

Ivan is still fighting off Rai as Kyle holds him with both his hands locked behind him. The moment Rai sees Reina, she abandons Ivan and runs toward me. I don't think twice. I don't even count as Kyle told me to.

I aim my gun, cock it, and then shoot straight into the fucker's chest. Kyle glares at me as Ivan falls limp in his hold. I ignore him and focus back on Reina.

Rai kneels beside her, begging her to open her eyes, demanding she keeps her promise.

Reina always said shit about wanting to leave, and this better not be the time she decides to do that.

I can't possibly live in a world without her anymore.

TWENTY-NINE

Reina

The end is a weird feeling.

It just…happens. Or maybe it doesn't happen and you're stuck somewhere in the unknown.

That's how it feels the moment I open my eyes. It's too quiet, too white, too full of nothingness. I think I'm in an afterlife of sorts. Everything ended in Ivan's torture chamber, and now I get to meet Mom and Dad.

But then the pain kicks in. It snaps from the back of my head to my temples. My eyes, which I thought I opened a second ago, are now half-open, drooping and…are they swollen?

I stick my tongue out to wet my dry lips and wince when it connects with tender, injured skin.

Then the smells register, strong and potent. Antiseptic and the cleanness of a hospital swallow my senses.

The sounds come into focus, too, as the blurriness slowly

fades away. A familiar face stares down at me. She's calling my name, tears welling in her eyes.

It's...*me*.

No, it's not me. It's Reina.

Oh, God. My heart picks up speed and the machines go mad with the beeping.

She can't be here. If she is, it could mean she's in the afterlife with me. She's—

"Doctor—call the doctor!"

A hand wraps around mine, warm and familiar, like Mom's. It feels just like Mom's.

The doctor shoves that light in front of my eyes and tells me to follow it. At first, I don't comply because I don't want to break eye contact with Reina. What if she disappears?

She nods at me, squeezing my hand encouragingly, so I follow the doctor's instructions. He asks me to talk and say my name.

"Reina," I whisper in a hoarse voice. "Reina Ellis."

A few people may know the fact that I'm not, but we promised I'd be Reina Ellis and she'd be Rai Sokolov. Until she takes back her life, I'll protect it. I'll do whatever it takes to keep it afloat.

Reina's face fills with so many emotions. My own would be similar if I could move it.

The doctor and the nurses fuss around Reina and me follows their every move, listening to the doctor and occasionally squeezing my hand to support it. The motions and the questions are almost a déjà vu of the last time I woke up in a similar bed with my memories wiped clean.

Only this time, it hurts more.

And this time...I slowly move my head around, but there's

no trace of Asher. A funny type of emptiness grips the center of my chest.

The doctor prescribes me some meds for the pain, and the nurse injects them into my IV. Then they leave, the door hissing closed behind them.

It's only Reina and me now.

Just like all those years ago.

She sits on the side of the bed, still holding my hand, careful not to jostle my side. From what the doctor said, I broke one rib and bruised two.

I'm scared to look at my face and witness all the damage Ivan has done.

"Is he dead?" I ask Reina.

She must realize exactly who I'm talking about since she nods tightly. "I stabbed him in the fucking eye."

"Good." My voice turns emotional. "Mom and Dad can rest in peace now."

I expected Reina to share my emotional reaction, but her expression hardens like a warrior before a battle. "I wish I did it earlier, but I couldn't hurt him. The leaders in Grandpa's closest chamber considered him the rightful heir, being a man and all. Ivan played a long-term game and made Mom and me appear like villains, like we brainwashed Grandpa. I had to get their blessing first, and I managed to persuade some strong allies, but the others wouldn't budge. When I heard about your kidnapping, though, I couldn't just stay still."

Allies and leaders...all this mafia talk comes out of Reina's mouth like it's second nature, like it's the only way she knows how to live.

"Will you..." I swallow. "Will you be okay now?"

She smiles a little. "Okay is my middle name, brat. You're the one who's always getting hurt."

"Well, I wasn't trained to stab people's eyes."

Her grin widens. "Grandpa taught me." Then her face falls. "I wish you could've met him. He was a hard man with a good core, but he just didn't know how to make Mom feel safe. That's why she ran away."

I gulp the saliva gathered at the back of my throat. "I think she ran away because she didn't want that life for us, Rei."

"Well, she didn't succeed. It's already too late." She strokes the back of my hand. "I have to go back to my world."

"Your world?" I choke and wince when my mouth aches.

"It is." She shrugs. "I won't let those who secretly allied with the fucker Ivan sully Grandpa's legacy. He trusted me with it, and it's my duty as a Sokolov to see it to the end."

"B-but we're talking about the mafia, Rei. The fucking mafia—they're deadly."

"I'm deadly, too. Grandpa didn't raise me to bow to those fucking pigs." Her shoulders straighten and her eyes lose their spark, turning cold and lethal. It's almost like an entirely different Reina.

She's not my sweet sister or the girl who trembled with me in the dark as we hid from Ivan's men. She now seems more like those men, if not more emotionless.

What have they done to my twin sister all these years? What have they turned her into?

"R-Reina, we promised to be together, remember?"

"And we will. We are." Her expression softens a little. "We'll just have to cross paths like Dad and I used to, you in your world and me in mine."

"No!" I shout, and my voice cracks. "That's not what we agreed on."

"We just promised to meet again." She raises an eyebrow. "We never agreed on anything else."

"Don't get smartass on me, Rei."

"It's the truth."

"Then…" I start to lick my lips then stop when I recall they're most likely busted and will hurt. "Then I'll go back to my identity and you go back to yours."

Truth is, being Rai Sokolov again scares the shit out of me. That little girl was a runaway, always hungry and empty. She was a shell of a person with no purpose in the world and no one to hold on to except for Mom, so when she was killed, I lost all sense of purpose.

Until I met Dad and Asher.

They gave me a reason to strive higher. That's why after Dad's death and Asher's disappearance, I became emptier again and let the gloomy cloud take over.

I only lived on the belief that I shouldn't screw up Reina's life because one day, she'd come back for it.

Today is that day where each of us takes back her life.

She gives me the side-eye. "You wouldn't survive a day in my world, Rai."

"Hey!"

"I'm serious. I wouldn't survive in your world either. It's too…normal. I can't do normal anymore."

"But—"

"No buts. You're Reina Ellis and I'm Rai Sokolov."

"You want me…" I cough on the lump in my throat. "You want me to be Reina?"

"You're already Reina. You just stop thinking about it as a role."

My lips part. "How did you…oh my God, you felt that way, too?"

She nods sharply. "I always thought it was just a role and I would need to give it back, but the last time we met, I realized how much you loved being Reina, and I've been meaning to tell you we should stop playing roles."

My mouth remains open as my brain struggles to find the right words to say. I didn't expect this at all and it just hits me out of nowhere.

"How…how about Asher? You know, the engagement and—"

She reaches into her pocket and retrieves a ring, a very familiar diamond ring. "I've been keeping it for you. I meant to come to find you after you were discharged at the hospital, but Kyle stopped me from seeing you since Ivan's men were watching."

"Kyle?"

"My bodyguard and right-hand man. He helped save you."

I'll have to thank him for it later.

"Anyway." She shoves the ring in my palm. "Here you go. I hate holding on to these precious things."

"But don't you want it?"

Her brows furrow. "Why the hell would I? I only wore it that day because you made me, saying it'd look great on me and shit. It doesn't. It's yours. Asher was never engaged to me, he was always engaged to you, Rai. I have no interest in him whatsoever."

Why have I thought she would? I always had the belief

Reina would demand to have him once she returned, that everything in my life belonged to her, not me.

But well, just because I'm so head over heels in love with Asher doesn't mean my twin would be.

A sense of relief engulfs me. It's like a weight has been lifted off my chest.

"Where…" I clear my throat. "Where is he?"

She's silent for a second as if trying to weigh her words. "He's not here."

The emptiness from earlier deepens and becomes a weight that nearly crushes my already injured ribcage. I hoped he'd be here for me as soon as I woke up.

We didn't even talk properly after we watched that video of Arianna and Jason.

"Then where is he?"

"Well, remember how I told you Ivan is dead?"

"Yeah, you stabbed him."

"In the eye, yes, but I wasn't the one who killed him. Asher put the bullet in the scum's chest."

I gasp then stop when pain shoots at the back of my neck.

As if being thrown into the depth of an ocean, my breathing disappears and I have to suck in air in order to feed my starved lungs.

"Is he…okay?"

"He's at the station with his father."

From what the doctor said earlier, I've been out for almost two days, so that should mean Asher has been away for the same length of time.

Oh, God. Does this mean he'll be convicted of murder? I can't have that fucker Ivan take another person away from me.

I try to sit up, but Reina makes me lie back down again.

"What are you doing?" she snaps.

"I have to go and help, I have to…do something. I can't just sit here."

"His father is with him. Alexander Carson is one of the best lawyers in the country, remember? He'll get him out of this. Besides, I made a statement and told them it was self-defense. Just rest, Rai. I'm sure Asher will be out in no time."

How can I rest when Asher's fate is unknown?

THIRTY

Reina

I can't rest.

The nurse has to sedate me so I'll close my eyes and sleep for the duration of the night.

The following day, the nurse and Reina help me wash up. The face I see in the mirror is too disfigured to be considered human. Purple and green bruises are scattered all over my skin; it's even worse than the previous time.

As I stare at it, I break down and cry. I hold on to the sink and let go of all the emotions I've been numbing for long years.

I cry for the little girl who had to run from one city to another, for the teenager who coveted someone she thought didn't belong to her, and for the woman who lost him all over again.

Asher and I always miss each other. Like parallel lines, it's almost as if we were never meant to cross paths. Whenever we do, a disaster occurs and we have to go back to that parallel existence, that helpless attempt to keep the order, and as a result, we become miserable.

At this point, I'm starting to think we're cursed. Maybe Arianna did some black magic before her death and made sure we'd never reunite.

The nurse pats my back, telling me none of my injuries will scar, that in a few weeks, it'll go back to the way it was.

She thinks I'm crying because of that, and it makes me cry harder. I don't stop until Reina comes inside and helps to wheel me back to bed.

It's then I notice the men in black standing in front of the door. In the beginning, I thought it was my security, but I don't spot Gaige and the others amongst them.

That's when I realize they must be Reina's people. She really does lead a different type of life.

"Are you better?" She takes the glass away after I swallow the pain pill the nurse gave me.

I shake my head as I close my eyes. I'll never be better until he's better.

It's crazy, but over time, Asher's wellbeing has begun to feel like my own.

Why don't they make a pain pill for the heart?

When I wake up again, it's dark. My throat is scratchy and dry.

A shadow sleeps on the chair beside me, which means Reina is staying the night again. She's barely left my side for the past two days. She only stepped out when Lucy, Naomi, Sebastian, Owen, and the cheerleading squad members visited.

Even they didn't know Asher's fate. The only information

available is that Alexander hasn't left his side. I've tried to call him, but his phone is always turned off.

Sitting up, I try to reach for the bottle and stop.

The body sitting on the chair isn't Reina's. She's not so broad and tall and...oh my God.

"Are you awake?" The tenor of his voice, that familiar deep tone makes me jolt.

"Asher?"

Please tell me this isn't a dream. It'd be the cruelest one yet.

Strong hands wrap around mine, and a sob catches in my throat.

It's Asher. Definitely Asher.

The way my skin bursts to life and how my body is attuned to his can't be mistaken.

Only he would elicit this reaction. It's not a dream or a hallucination; it's reality.

"I'm here, prom queen. You can't get rid of me that easily."

"It's really you." My voice is haunted by the force of my emotions. "What happened? Are they letting you go?"

"Alexander managed to have them rule it as self-defense. Rai's testimony helped."

"Thank God. I thought you...you'd be locked up."

"And leave you up for grabs? Not going to happen, prom queen." Under the soft light coming from the window behind me, he appears exhausted, his face worn out. He must've not slept for days, but he still came here the moment he was released. That warms my heart and allows little butterflies to explode in my stomach.

"Are you okay?" I can't help asking.

"I'm fine, but are you?" He stares at me, and even in the

dark, I feel his gaze swallowing me whole. Being in the center of Asher's attention is like that, overwhelming and uncut.

He reaches a hand to my face but stops midway, clenching it into a fist and letting it drop to his lap. "I should've killed that fucker slower."

It should scare me that he's thinking about murder and ending lives, but I hated Ivan too much to care. Besides, Asher always had this side to him, ever since high school, the side that needs to hurt and maim, the side that was once unleashed on me.

But he stopped himself; he always stopped himself when it came to me. A part of him might have wanted to kill me because of the grudge Arianna left between us, but the other part couldn't stop wanting to be close to me.

"Reina or Rai or whoever you want to be." His hold on my hand tightens as he straightens and lowers his voice. "I fucked up. I know I did and it was bad. I can lie to you and say I never wanted to hurt you, but that would be a lie and I promised myself I'd never lie to you again. So here's the uncensored version, prom queen. I wanted to hurt you. I thought if I hurt you, if I erased you from this world, then it would stop the fucking urge that's been gripping me for three years. But the closer I got to my goal, the emptier it felt. It was even more fucking pathetic than in high school when I was beating people up for talking to you. When I watched you hanging from the roof that day, I wanted to keep you, and since then, with everything I did, you stood back up, and that made me want to have you more.

"That's what I want to do with you all the time, Reina. I want to dominate you, hurt you, but only so I can hear you scream in pleasure. I want to keep you, to have you, to play games with you, *not* against you. If you want nothing to do with me, it'd be the smarter choice. No one would blame you."

I stare at him after he finishes talking. His words hit a deep place inside me that's been yearning for something like that, for something true and raw from him.

He's still a psycho in some ways and I can't completely forgive what he did to me, how he tormented me, but I can see why he was compelled to do it. I can also see how he stopped every time.

I can also see the boy I used to sit with because his presence tuned down the chaos from the outside world. He made it safe and pleasant and then I had to screw him over and act cold because I was scared of him, of what he was offering, of what I've been feeling.

Yes, I could make him grovel for what he did, I could delay this and hold on and make him fall to his knees. But when Ivan was beating me up, I had an epiphany: life is too short to delay things. You never know what will happen tomorrow, so the present is all you get to make a difference.

Besides, he can grovel while he's glued to my side.

"Just so you know," he says when I remain silent, "if you do want to stay away, I can't promise I will. I'll keep trying until you'll have me again."

"What if I don't?" I keep my voice nonchalant.

"I'll keep trying until you take me."

"I love you, Ash. I always have." The words slip out of me so easily, it's baffling that I never said them out loud before.

He pauses, his breathing turning harsh, almost animalistic. "Always?"

"Always."

"Even when you were cold and standoffish?"

I laugh. "Especially when I was cold and standoffish. It was a façade, Ash. The deeper my feelings ran for you, the harder I tried to kill them."

He's quiet for a second as if mulling my words over. When he speaks, my heart stops beating. "I love you, too, Reina. You're my first and last."

"You're my first and last too." I retrieve the ring Reina gave me. "Now, give me a decent proposal, because I don't remember the last one."

EPILOGUE

Reina
Five years later

" A sh...Ash..."

"What is it, prom queen?" He slows down, his hips rolling in an unhurried rhythm as he pins my throat to the ground.

He's fucking me from the side at the entrance. The moment I walked into our apartment, he grabbed me by the throat and wrapped his other hand around my eyes, making the world black and more...thrilling.

Then he threw me to the ground, tore my clothes off like a caveman, and made me lie on my side so he could fuck me deep and fast.

It's a game we sometimes play, the unknown. It always makes me so wanton and I come harder than ever before.

Asher's intense side is my heaven. With each touch and stroke, I fall deeper and harder for him.

In public, I'm his queen; in bed, I'm his most obedient slut, the one he pleasures every night and in the morning before we go to work.

His hand never leaves my throat as he rams into me. His arm crushes my breast, making my nipples throb with the need to be bitten, touched, and tortured by him.

Now, of all times, he slows his pace. He can't just leave me hanging after all that build-up; I'm about to explode.

"Harder, you fucking asshole."

He laughs, the sound harsh and dark. "That's not how it works. Say the words."

Usually, all I have to do is say 'please', but today, I'm aching for a strong release, so I say, "I'm yours, only yours, Ash."

"Yes, you are," he grunts as he thickens inside me until I can feel him stretch me all over again. He slides out almost entirely then slams back in again.

Once.

Twice.

The third time, my nails dig into his arm as my lips part in a wordless cry.

The release crashes into me as he captures my mouth in a ravenous kiss and pounds into me harder and faster. My pulse heightens and my whimpers are shaky with the strength of it.

I can't breathe. No, I don't want to breathe.

I want to take him in at his rawest form, all uncut and mine. My best friend, my husband, and my number one supporter.

His kiss turns breathless and out of control as his cum fills me. We both sigh into each other's mouth at the same time, but we don't stop kissing.

His hand strokes my throat as he opens my mouth and

fucks my tongue with his. I don't know how long we remain on the carpet as he kisses the ever-loving daylights out of me.

All I know is that I become too sleepy and exhausted; he always has that effect on me. Every time he thoroughly fucks me, I sleep like a baby afterward—that is if he doesn't wake me up in the middle of the night for another round.

He slips out of me and I moan at the emptiness as his cum streaks between my thighs. I love this feeling a bit too much.

As always, Asher carries me in his arms toward our bedroom. I lean over and suck on the skin of his neck, kissing along it with everything I have.

"Careful there, prom queen—you're asking for it again." He smirks down at me.

I hit his chest. "Stop it."

He has aged like a fine wine, still as attractive as sin, if not a bit more lethal. Now, women don't leave him alone. I'm always tempted to shove the wedding ring in their faces.

I don't need to, though. Asher has never looked at another woman. Hell, he barely has time to take care of work and meet up with his friends due to his fixation on me. I've lost count of the number of times I've found him watching me intently, as if he doesn't believe we're actually together.

Truth is, I watch him that way too when I know he's not looking. We were always parallel lines, but even parallel lines can collide and become one. It's even more powerful than two lines meeting at only one point.

He places me down and lies beside me. He pulls me on top of him so my breasts are glued to his chest, my legs between his and my face inches away from his.

Another position I love too much to admit.

We watch each other for a second, his hands running

through my hair and mine stroking along his tattoo. The Arabic words are still there, and I'm glad he didn't remove it. I like to see how far we've come.

Jason has admitted to helping Arianna back then, and he was also the one behind that shady Instagram account about Blackwood College. He had students DM him pictures and he posted them.

After that confrontation, he got a beating from Asher that nearly broke his football arm. When Alex found out about what happened, he wanted to throw Jason out of the country, but I begged him not to for Izzy's sake. She showed me that video when she could've kept it a secret for life because she cared about Alex and me.

She offered to take Jason and go back to the south where her family would deal with him.

I could tell Asher wanted to do more than beat Jason up, but I made him stop. I had a few choice words for Jason. I thought he was my friend, but he turned out to be my worst enemy. However, I didn't waste my time on him—it wasn't worth it after everything that happened.

The past isn't something we should dwell on; the future is.

We won state that year, or more like Lucy and Prescott did. Their management of the team while I was recovering was amazing. Now, they're happily married and running a dance studio.

Owen went on to the NFL, and Asher and I usually go watch him play. He's such a star that we need a pass to see him.

Sebastian and Naomi—well, it's complicated, as Naomi likes to say.

Rai has remained in her world and made a name for herself in the bratva.

We often meet, but it has to be pre-scheduled and monitored since she leads a dangerous life and needs to keep a low profile.

I call her Rai and she calls me Reina now. We decided to do that about four years ago. It was useless to keep that promise from when we were kids. We're just us now. Rai Sokolov and Reina Carson.

Reina Carson.

I fall in love with that name the more I think about it.

We got married within a year. Asher told me in no uncertain terms that he'd waited too long to have me so now the waiting was over.

I continued my master's degree in sociology, and now I help children like me, runways without a home and sometimes no support.

Asher started working for Alexander's company after finishing his degree in international law. I can't say father and son see eye to eye on everything, but they tolerate each other better. Learning the truth about Arianna's death set them both free, since they'd been secretly blaming each other.

We usually meet for dinners with Alex. He's still the best father figure I could've had. He walked me down the aisle on Dad's behalf on my wedding day.

"I thought you were going to sleep." Asher raises an eyebrow.

Okay, so I might have been watching him like a creep for the few last seconds...or minutes. Whatever.

"Hey, Ash."

"Hmm?"

Ash has become his favorite name now. I smile to myself

remembering how he used to be creeped out by it, or maybe he was creeped out by that side of me.

Once, I was acting like a brat and kept calling him Asher. His reaction was fucking me in the ass until I screamed Ash.

It's his way or the highway, and I love every second of it.

"I want kids." It's unplanned, but it's not spur of the moment. I've been thinking about this for a while.

At the beginning of our marriage, we agreed to delay having kids for our careers, but now I want to carry his baby.

"The idea of you pregnant makes me hard." He pushes into me, nuzzling the evidence between my thighs.

"It turns me on, too." I bite my lower lip.

"That's my prom queen." He captures my lips in a kiss as he parts my thighs with a strong hand.

His slides inside me with that slight pressure that makes me quiver, ready for him all over again.

"Ash," I whisper against his mouth. "I'm sleepy."

"You can't bring up the idea of pregnancy then be sleepy." He brushes his lips against mine. "I won't stop until I put a baby inside you."

God, this man.

I love him so much, it's mad.

You can read about Rai, Reina's twin sister, and Kyle in *Throne of Power*.

Curious about Asher's friend, Aiden? Get *Deviant King* and find out what happens when she provokes the school's most popular boy.

WHAT'S NEXT?

Thank you so much for reading *All The Truths*! If you liked it, please leave a review!

Your support means the world to me.

If you're thirsty for more discussions with other readers of the series, you can join Rina's Spoilers Room.

If you're searching for your next thrilling read from Rina Kent, check out the recommended reading order.

ALSO BY RINA KENT

For more books by the author and a reading order, please visit:

www.rinakent.com/books

ABOUT THE AUTHOR

Rina Kent is a *USA Today*, international, and #1 Amazon bestselling author of everything enemies to lovers romance.

She's known to write unapologetic anti-heroes and villains because she often fell in love with men no one roots for. Her books are sprinkled with a touch of darkness, a pinch of angst, and an unhealthy dose of intensity.

She spends her private days in London laughing like an evil mastermind about adding mayhem to her expanding universe. When she's not writing, Rina travels, hikes, and spoils cats in a pure Cat Lady fashion.

Find Rina Below:

Website: www.rinakent.com

Newsletter: www.subscribepage.com/rinakent

BookBub: www.bookbub.com/profile/rina-kent

Amazon: www.amazon.com/Rina-Kent/e/B07MM54G22

Goodreads: www.goodreads.com/author/show/18697906.Rina_ Kent

Instagram: www.instagram.com/author_rina

Facebook: www.facebook.com/rinaakent

Reader Group: www.facebook.com/groups/rinakent.club

Pinterest: www.pinterest.co.uk/AuthorRina/boards

Tiktok: www.tiktok.com/@rina.kent

Twitter: twitter.com/AuthorRina